One Moonlit Night

Reviewers and reader's comments:

"I definitely enjoyed this novel. Well written and fast-paced plot!"
The International Review of Books

"One Moonlit Night by Donna F. Brown is one of the finest fiction thrillers I have ever read. The book is a real page turner, and an intriguing read that left me craving for more."
Pratibha Malav – Book Reviewer@pratibhaloveswriting

Donna writes of loving relationships and mortal threats with engaging detail. She makes sure there is never a moment to rest as we follow the lives of her characters through the harrowing story. One Moonlit Night is a page-turner.
Donn Poll – Artist and Mystery Reader

"The aspect that I loved most about this book is the excellent plot development. I found the various parts of the plot steadily developed, an attribute that ensured my enjoyment of the story… There is absolutely nothing that I liked least about this intricate tale. I, therefore, believe that this masterpiece merits a full rating of five out of five stars."
Helen Muriithi – Professional Book Reviewer at Amazon, Goodreads, and OnlineBookClub.org

"When you pick up "One Moonlit Night" don't make any other plans for a few hours, because you won't want to put it down! Lots of intrigue, interesting characters, and mystery make it a real page-turner – you won't get it out of your mind for days!"
Kathleen Harris – Retired Attorney, Musician

One
Moonlit
Night
Donna F. Brown
G & D Publishing
Pearce, Arizona

Publisher's Cataloging-in-Publication data

Names: Brown, Donna F., author.
Title: One Moonlit Night / by Donna F. Brown.
Description: Pearce, AZ: G&D Publishing, 2021.
Identifiers: LCCN: 2021905674 |
ISBN: 978-1-7368552-0-1 (paperback) |
    978-1-7368552-1-8 (e-book)
Subjects: LCSH United States. Marine Corps--Officials and
employees--Fiction. | Murder--Fiction. | Mystery fiction. |
Thriller fiction. | BISAC FICTION / Thrillers / Psychological |
FICTION / Mystery & Detective / General
Classification: LCC PS3602.R6955 O54 2021 | DDC 813.6--dc23

ISBN: Paperback 978-1-7368552-0-1
ISBN: eBook 978-1-7368552-1-8
LCCN: 2021905674

ACKNOWLEDGEMENTS

I would like to acknowledge my husband, Gary Brown, who was a tremendous help and support throughout the writing and publishing of this novel. He continues to be a never-ending source of ideas, always willing to lend an ear (or two) to listen to my ideas, a shoulder to lean on, and a welcoming port in every storm. Without his love, support, and encouragement, this novel might never have been written.

Thanks also to Donn Poll, Art Director/Designer at A3D Impressions, Inc. for his superb artwork design and layout of the front and back covers of this novel. I appreciate his proofreading skills and creative ideas for ways to make the story come alive.

Thanks also to Maureen Sangiorgio, Award-winning Writer, NRA-certified Firearms Instructor/RSO, for her professional editing of this book. I truly appreciate her professionalism, thoroughness and support of my writing this story.

A warm thank you goes out to Rick Wamer, my previous publisher, for his endless support and encouragement throughout my book writing journey.

Another hearty thank you to Rona Baker, retired secondary education English teacher, for her generous time devoted to copy editing this book.

PROLOGUE

One moonlit night, the snow-covered forest was as still as the lull before a storm with only an intermittent, chilly breeze blowing. A brilliantly shining moon hung in the sky, illuminating a section of the footpath that wound its way through the forest.

A dark, shadowy figure crouched on all fours behind a gnarly, old oak tree and peered up at the moon. As was his usual routine, the figure would roam around in the darkness of the densely wooded forest with superb night vision. Gazing up at the moon, the figure turned his body from the light and crept deeper into the forest.

Standing now fully erect at six feet tall, he lingered for a few moments near an open field. Running a hand through his wavy brown hair, he took in the surrounding silence. The forest provided a welcome reprieve from invasive memories and brief visions flashing through his mind. The visions occurred with predictable regularity since that fateful night one month ago when he ran from the house out into the eerie darkness of that mid-winter night. Visions and sounds of flashing police lights and sirens flooded his anguished brain. He held a gloved hand up to his hazel eyes to shield them from the nightmarish images…

CHAPTER 1
(Sunday, February 21, 2016)

Dan Stevens sat on a comfortable light brown sofa in his Cape Cod style home in Archer, Vermont in front of a blazing fire burning in the fireplace. The hour was late and he was the only one awake.

His wife, Peggy, sister Gina, and two young daughters, Annie and Stephanie, had already gone upstairs to bed. Gazing intently at the wildly flickering flames, he felt his eyelids getting heavier with each passing second. Glancing at the clock on the wall, he noticed it was a few minutes after midnight.

Recalling the conversation he had with his sister, Gina, earlier that evening, he smiled. She had invited him to join her and her husband, Wes, both avid cross-country skiers, at a ski resort the following year in Keystone, Colorado. Gina worked part-time for him as a receptionist at the architecture business he took over from his dad after his death five years ago. Wes worked long hours as a research chemist and commuted on weekdays to his job in the city of Montview, about an hour's drive from Archer.

When serving his country in Afghanistan for four years with the U.S. Marine Corps in his early twenties, Dan was very active. He remained active after leaving the Marines. He ran three to five miles daily and downhill skied in the Green Mountains near his hometown of Archer.

When he met Peggy in his late twenties, he settled into married life and became more sedentary. When not working at his architecture company, he enjoyed painting watercolor landscapes and doing a bit of writing. He scanned the room, and he gazed down at the carefully sanded and brown-stained wooden floor planks. He smiled and remembered his dad who taught him the fine art of architecture and design. He glanced around the room admiring his colorful landscape paintings that added a decorative touch to sandstone colored walls. One winter scene he created caught his attention and reminded him of Gina.

His smile widened as he thought of himself stumbling around on cross country skis, yet he looked forward to a lesson offered by Gina. They usually got along famously, and anytime spent with Gina was quality time.

Rising from the couch, he strolled over to the fireplace and gazed down into the slowly dying embers. Throwing another log onto the embers, he stirred the fire with a poker and soon the flames blazed with a new intensity. Heading back toward the couch, he lay down and soon fell asleep.

A man of medium height and muscular build wearing a long black trench coat and full black face mask slowly approached the two story house and gazed up at the dark upstairs bedroom windows. Satisfied the family was asleep, he turned his attention to the lit downstairs windows and silently crept toward them. Peering in through one window, he scanned the front room and its contents. He took notice of the layout: two recliner chairs with a lamp and table between them, and a sofa with its side facing toward the window. A tan throw pillow on the couch was obstructing his view, so he couldn't tell if anyone was sitting or lying on the couch. He tried to open the window, but it was locked. Walking over to the door, he slowly turned the knob and to his great delight, discovered it was not locked. *That was easy,* he thought. He grinned and entered the house.

Silently making his way through the front room he passed behind the sofa, unaware of the man asleep on the other side. His attention was focused on the stairway leading to the upstairs bedrooms. Cautiously creeping up the side of the stairs, he approached the guest room, and observing the door wide open, peeked in and saw it was empty.

Continuing down the hallway, he now stood in front of another bedroom and noticing a few stick figure paintings taped to the door, he knew this was where the girls slept. Entering their room, he carefully approached the beds and pulled a penlight and knife out of his coat pocket. Silvery slivers of moonlight sliced through the sheer pink curtains on the windows, and silhouetted the small sleeping figures of the two girls. Shining his penlight on the girl in the bed nearest where he stood, he stared at her freckled face and strawberry blond hair and smiled. *You will be first, little one,* he thought. *All good girls go to heaven.*

Turning off the penlight and placing it back in his pocket, he reached his gloved hand toward the sleeping child and covered her mouth. Suddenly her eyes flew open and stared at him in wide-eyed terror. Before she could let out a muffled cry, he stabbed her repeatedly with the knife until her small body squirmed no more.

Hearing a noise behind him, he turned and saw the other girl sneaking toward the doorway. He reached out and grabbed her by her long auburn hair and threw her down on the floor. Pouncing on her, he covered her mouth and muffled her yell for help. His knife found its bloody mark once again. Satisfied the girls were both dead, he left their room and headed for the master bedroom.

Quickly scanning the hallway to assure himself there was no one around, he entered the last bedroom and approached the bed where the woman was fast asleep. Hearing her heavy breathing, he held the knife above her for a few brief seconds studying the details of her peaceful face as she slept. *Sleep well, sweetheart, for all eternity,* he mumbled softly under his breath. The man now covered her mouth and with a glint in his dark, evil eyes, and a sinister smile on his face, his knife slashed through his next victim.

Dan was suddenly awakened by the loud thump he heard coming from upstairs. Sitting upright, he shook the sleep from his eyes and listened for a few moments, yet heard only silence. Wondering what he heard, he got up from the sofa and headed upstairs.

Walking down the hallway toward his and Peggy's bedroom, he passed the guestroom where Gina slept and noticed the door was open. Knowing his sister, he thought that was rather strange, as she always kept her door closed when in her room. Peering cautiously into the room, he discovered she was nowhere to be found.

Entering the room, he called her name, yet heard no response. Scanning the room, he saw a note lying on her bed. Holding the note in his hand, it read,

"*Hey Dan,*

I just remembered something I wanted to give you that was left back at the house (silly me), and as it's late and you're still sleeping, I'll just stay at my house tonight and call you in the morning. Thanks for a great evening and conversation!"

Love,

Gina

Putting the note in his shirt pocket, he walked out of her room and continued making his way toward the bedroom his daughters shared. Pausing for a few moments, he gazed lovingly at the watercolor drawings his daughters had taped on the door. When he was painting, he enjoyed having them with him painting their own pictures.

He envisioned the beaming faces of Annie, who had just turned eight, and Stephanie, a mere six years of age, running toward him to show off their pictures just a few days prior.

Smiling at the memory, he slowly opened the door and quietly stepped inside so as not to wake them. Seeing the silhouette of Stephanie lying absolutely still in her bed was at first comforting, until he noticed Annie's bed was empty. Suddenly, a strong unmistakable odor of metal and rust hit him full on. In a panic, he turned on the light switch. Dan held his breath as he approached Stephanie's bed. The sight that met his eyes went far beyond his most horrific nightmares.

He noticed Stephanie was covered with blood on her chest and face. She stared sightlessly at him with her mouth agape as if still trying to scream. Yelling her name, he placed his fingers on her neck and checked for a pulse. Unable to find a pulse, he started CPR on her. After a few minutes, he rushed over to Annie's inert, bloody body lying on the floor and tried to revive her. After several more minutes, he saw no signs of life in either of his daughters. "Dear God! NO," he wept as he gathered the bloodied bodies of his beloved daughters in his arms.

He suddenly heard another loud thump coming from the master bedroom, and now in full panic mode, he sprinted down the hallway. Crashing through the closed door, he flipped on the light switch and discovered Peggy's bloodied and battered body lying on the floor.

Gasping in open-mouthed horror, he saw a man in a black trench coat brandishing a knife and trying to escape through the open window. In a flash, Dan dashed toward the intruder, grabbed him by the collar of his coat and pulled him back into the bedroom. Instantly, the intruder turned and charged toward him, slicing the air with his knife mere inches from Dan's face. Standing face to face, Dan stared into the intruder's evil eyes and was momentarily stunned by the intensity of his sinister glare. He knew he was in for the fight of his life.

Grabbing the intruder's arm holding the knife, he tried to knock it out of his hand and with his fist landed a full on punch on the intruder's jaw. The intruder stumbled backwards a few steps, but once again charged toward Dan, throwing his full weight on him and knocking him to the floor.

In a matter of seconds, the intruder landed on top of him holding his knife to Dan's throat. He felt the cold steel blade grazing his throat. With every ounce of strength he had, he grabbed the intruder's hand and forcefully pushed it away from his throat. Dan kept pushing the intruder's arm backwards past its normal range of motion and kneed him in the groin. Wincing in pain, the intruder dropped the knife and it slid across the floor a few feet away from where they lie. Seeing his opportunity, Dan flipped the intruder on his back with him on top. He repeatedly punched the intruder's face and knocked him out cold.

Dan dragged himself off the unconscious man, and was overcome with exhaustion and overwhelming grief. He staggered over to where Peggy was lying and dropped to the floor on his knees. Gathering his wife into his arms, he rocked her back and forth, hot tears relentlessly pouring from his eyes. "Peggy," he sobbed the desolate despair of one who has given up all hope. "I'm so sorry! I'm so sorry I wasn't here to protect you!" He gently caressed her bloodied face with his fingers and brushed her tangled hair away from her face.

His grieving was suddenly interrupted by a deep, raspy voice coming from behind him. "Hey! Remember me?" Dan whirled around to face the intruder who had blood streaming from his nose and mouth and was wielding the knife. He sprang to his feet just in time to lift his arm and block the intruder from stabbing him in his chest. He winced in pain as the knife sliced his right shoulder. He ran full sprint into the intruder, knocking him again to the floor.

"You son of a bitch! You need to die, asshole!" Grabbing his feet, he dragged the man out of the bedroom, down the hallway toward the stairs. Dan yanked him up to a standing position and pushed him down the stairs. Watching his assailant lying motionless in a crumpled heap at the bottom of the stairs, he ran back into the bedroom, opened the nightstand drawer, pulled out a Smith & Wesson SD and dashed toward the stairway. Holding his gun out in front of him and reaching the stairway, he peered down the stairs just in time to see one of the assailant's legs disappear out the front door.

Bolting down the stairs, Dan ran outside, stopping to catch his breath and scan the area for any signs of the intruder. He saw no one. His breath ragged and panting, his heart broken, he stood in the driveway staring into the darkness and emptiness of his soul.

CHAPTER 2
(Sunday, February 21, 2016)

After calling 911, Dan sat with his head in his hands on a chair in the front room that faced the same window the intruder had peered through just hours before. In a daze, his eyes devoid of tears, he glanced toward the clock on the wall above the fireplace and noticed it was now 1:30 a.m. His mind was flooded with thoughts of the conversations with Peggy and his daughters earlier in the evening.

Peggy and he had been sitting on the couch and Dan had his arm around her shoulders. They were anticipating their vacation in Hawaii the following week, and were talking excitedly about their plans to do some snorkeling and swim with the dolphins. Peggy, an avid swimmer and hiker, had talked him into trying these activities, as she had a more adventurous spirit than he did. They were also looking forward to doing some parasailing and enjoying a dinner cruise afterwards.

Annie and Stephanie were sitting on the floor absorbed in watching a movie featuring their favorite character, a sloth. They would laugh hysterically every time the sloth appeared. Dan and Peggy had discussed taking them along, yet both had been working long hours at their jobs and wanted to spend some quality time alone. Gina had offered to watch the children for the week Dan and Peggy would be away, and they were grateful for her offer.

Stephanie's birthday was a few weeks away and Gina had privately mentioned to Dan that she had bought a gift for her, yet forgot it back at her house. Gina and Wes had no children of their own, except for a very lovable and active border collie, Harley. Gina picked the name from her love of riding with Wes on his Harley motorcycle. Harley had her own little dog caddy that Wes attached to a special hitch on the back of his motorcycle.

Suddenly, remembering that Gina had left the house before the murders, he tried calling her number on his cell and heard her recorded message. "Hey Gina, it's Dan… I need to talk to you right away…"

The sound of sirens and flashing lights on the driveway jolted him back to the present, so he ended the call. Waiting the ten minutes since his 911 call seemed like hours. Bolting outside into the chilly February night, wearing only a torn, blood-stained t-shirt and jeans, he greeted the sheriff and deputy who were the first to arrive on the scene. Sheriff Tom Anderson was the first to get out of the squad car and met Dan halfway up the driveway. They both shook hands and he introduced his Deputy, Joe Warner.

A light snow was falling and the cold, wet crystal snowflakes landed on Dan's bare skin, sending slight shivers up his spine. An ambulance with its siren blaring arrived shortly after the sheriff, and two paramedics ran out of the vehicle and approached Dan. He motioned with his hand toward the upstairs bedroom windows and the paramedics ran into the house and disappeared from sight.

Within a few seconds, another squad car arrived, two officers jumped out and nodding at Dan, they rushed past him through the open doorway of the house.

After greetings and offers of condolences from the sheriff and deputy, they slowly walked up the driveway with Dan and entered the house.

Dan was the first to enter, followed by the sheriff and deputy. Following him into the front room, they took their seats in the two cozy, neutrally-colored recliner chairs on either side of the ornately-carved, dark brown lamp table. Dan wearily sat down on the light brown sofa that had been present since first buying the house eight years prior, when Peggy was pregnant with Annie, their firstborn child. He absent-mindedly ran his fingers over the slightly faded and well-worn corduroy cushions and waited for the sheriff to start the inquiry.

Dan gazed across the room at the sheriff and studied him for a few moments. He appeared to be pushing fifty, tall, with a sturdy athletic build and sandy brown hair with greying temples. The deputy appeared to be around the same age as the sheriff, although not as tall and heavier set. He wore a frown on his face and his dark brown eyes nervously darted around the room as if he were waiting for Satan himself to appear. Every few minutes, he would write down some notes on his clipboard.

Sheriff Anderson focused his penetrating blue eyes on Dan. "So, tell me Dan, exactly what happened here?" Dan paused for a few moments to gather his wits before he spoke. "Peggy and the girls were already in bed and I was asleep here on the couch…" Barely speaking in a whisper, he recounted everything he could remember about finding his wife and daughters stabbed to death and the fight that ensued between himself and the intruder.

Listening to Dan's story, the sheriff nodded and when Dan paused to regain his composure, he asked, "Do you have any idea who the perpetrator is or what his motive could have been?" Visions of the intruder trying to escape through the bedroom window suddenly flooded his mind. His eyes filled with tears as he stared down at the floor. "I don't have a clue who the guy was. Peggy has always been such a caring and loving person, I can't think of anyone who would want to kill her. And, who in their right mind would kill children?"

The sheriff continued his investigation. "Dan, I know how difficult this is, yet I need you to describe him to the best of your knowledge. How tall, how much did he weigh, color of his hair and eyes…"

Suddenly, there was a knock at the door and another law enforcement agent entered. "Sheriff, sorry to interrupt, but there's a woman outside named Gina, and…" Before he finished his sentence, Dan jumped up from the couch and running toward the officer he replied, "That's my sister! Where is she?" The officer pointed toward the driveway that was now covered with squad cars. Signaling back to the sheriff, he left the house.

Running outside behind the officer, Dan noticed several other officers were yellow taping the perimeter of his house.

They were also trying to calm a number of neighbors who were standing in the street wondering what the commotion was all about. Archer was a fairly small town in which most of the action that occurred was an occasional bar fight. The neighbors were now alarmed by all the squad cars outside Dan's house.

Scanning the growing crowd of onlookers, he noticed his next door neighbors, Dorothy and Jim Mueller, waving at him trying to get his attention. Nodding in their direction, he saw a petite woman with glasses and light brown hair standing in front of them, yelling his name. He recognized his sister, Gina. He also saw a short, wiry man with steel grey, short-cropped hair standing next to her, and realized it was Wes, her husband. Running toward her and Wes, he noticed an officer was attempting to hold them behind the yellow crime scene tape. Reaching them, he informed the officer who they were. They all embraced in a group hug and lingered for several seconds.

After their long embrace, Gina turned to face Dan with tears streaming from her eyes, and was the first to speak. "I got your message and heard the urgency in your voice." She looked directly at him and asked with concern, "Where are Peggy and the girls? Are they alright?" Dan shook his head and stared at the ground. "They are… dead, Gina," he whispered. Stunned, Gina stared at him in wide-eyed horror and disbelief. "WHAT??? Oh dear God, Dan, what are you saying?"

Dan tearfully repeated his story about the intruder and his ordeal. "We should continue this conversation inside, Dan," Wes replied, patting Dan's good shoulder. Dan nodded and headed toward the house with Gina and Wes following behind. Wes, stunned by Dan's revelation, nervously glanced back at the crowd of people in the street while officers held them behind the yellow tape surrounding the property. He had an eerie feeling that someone was watching them, but not seeing anyone unfamiliar, he shrugged it off. A few more neighbors called out to Dan, yet he was not in the mood to respond.

The three of them entered into the front room. The sheriff and deputy stood up from their chairs and shook hands with Gina and Wes as Dan introduced them. They sat back down in their chairs and Gina and Wes sat next to Dan on the couch.

"So, I'm sure Dan filled you both in on what happened," the sheriff declared, glancing at Gina and Wes. They solemnly nodded their affirmation. "Let's continue then. Dan, we were previously talking about the perpetrator, and you were about to describe him to the best of your knowledge."

"I… I know he was rather muscular, roughly around five foot nine or ten and…" he paused to scan his memory for further details. "He was wearing a long black trench coat, a black face mask and dark gloves. They could have been either black or brown. I couldn't really tell in the moment." He deeply sighed and glancing up at the clock, noticed it was almost 3 a.m. Feeling exhausted and grief-stricken, he slumped back into the sofa cushion to rest his body. Gina reached over and patted Dan's hand reassuringly.

"Do you remember anything else about him?" asked Deputy Warner looking up from his clipboard.

"His eyes. Those dark eyes were intense and full of hatred. I don't ever recall seeing eyes so terrifying and remorseless."

His whispered words hung momentarily suspended in

mid-air, interrupted by the sound of heavy footsteps hurrying down the stairs. An officer entered the front room holding a large plastic bag in his hand containing a bloodied object. He walked over to the sheriff. "You might want to take a look at this," the officer said and handed the bag to the sheriff. They talked for a brief moment and the officer walked back upstairs.

All eyes were on the sheriff as he carefully examined the contents of the bag. After a few moments of contemplation, he rose from the chair, and walked over to where Dan sat on the couch. Holding the bag in front of Dan, he asked, "Is this the weapon the perpetrator used to kill your wife and daughters?" Dan gravely studied the bloody dagger for a brief moment and nodded his head. "Yes, that's the knife he used." Gina uttered a moan and tightly clutched Wes's hand. "Oh my God," she cried and leaned her head to rest on Wes' shoulder. Wes wrapped his arms around Gina and held her as she sobbed uncontrollably into his shirt.

The sheriff glanced at Gina as she wiped her eyes with a tissue she pulled from her purse.

"Gina, I know this is difficult for you, yet I need to ask Dan a few more questions to assist us in finding and bringing this criminal to justice. So, is it okay if we proceed now?"

"I'm sorry, sheriff," Gina interjected, "I just can't believe something this horrible has happened to my brother and our family!" Gina reached again for Dan's hand and held it tightly in hers. Dan leaned over and they embraced for a few moments. Pulling slowly away from her, he motioned to the sheriff with his hand. "Ask away…" his voice trailed off.

"Is that your gun?" he asked pointing to the Smith & Wesson lying on the lamp table. "Yes, after fighting with the guy, I threw him down the stairs and ran back into the bedroom for the gun to protect myself if he tried to attack me again." He remembered laying the gun on the lamp table when he returned to the house after the guy took off.

"Did you notice if anything was stolen?"

"No, sheriff, I didn't. As I previously told you, I was focused on trying to catch the guy after he fled. I haven't yet had a chance to check."

"Did Peggy or your daughters have any enemies, or did they have any arguments or fights with anyone recently or in the past?" Dan pondered his question for a few moments. "I suppose Annie might have had a few spats with some classmates in the playground after school, yet nothing serious where someone would want to kill her. Stephanie had just started kindergarten last fall." Trying to regain his composure, he continued. "Peggy was an upstanding member of our community, church, and even worked part-time as an aide at the children's school. I don't recall her having any fights or arguments with anyone."

"I know it's late, Dan. I have one last question. Did you and Peggy ever get into any arguments recently?" Dan shook his head. "We've had our little quarrels here and there as everyone does, yet again, nothing where I'd want to do her any harm. Earlier this evening, we were talking about leaving next week on our vacation in Hawaii…"

Suddenly, one of the paramedics appeared at the top of the stairs and called out to Dan. "Sir, could you please come upstairs for a minute?" Dan exchanged glances with Gina and Wes. He slowly walked upstairs and followed the paramedic back to the girls' bedroom and steadied himself outside the room for a brief moment before entering.

One paramedic was standing next to Stephanie's bed and Dan noticed her body was covered with a sheet. There were several officers talking with the paramedic. The other paramedic signaled for him to come over to where Annie lie on her back on the floor.

Dan knelt over her and saw she had electrodes attached to her chest and an oxygen mask on her face. He was stunned to see her chest rising and falling intermittently as the AED machine was detecting a fluttering heartbeat.

"Oh dear Lord… is she alive?" Dan gasped and reached out his hand to touch her face.

"Sir, please step back for a moment," the paramedic held out his arm to stop Dan from touching his daughter, as the portable defibrillator machine next to Annie had just delivered a shock to her heart. Dan waited in silence, barely breathing. The AED announced that Annie's heartbeat had been converted to a normal rhythm.

"Is she going to be OK?" Dan pressed the paramedic for some reassurance.

"We're going to get her to the hospital right away and they will take over. She's stable for now. You can ride with us. Let's go!" declared the paramedic. With a quick glance at Stephanie's sheet-covered body, Dan realized he barely had a chance to grieve her loss. Wiping more tears from his face, he turned his attention to the paramedics carrying Annie in a litter out of the bedroom and followed them out.

When Dan was back downstairs, he saw the officers who were in Annie's room talking with the sheriff and deputy, and updating them with news about Annie. Gina and Wes hurried toward Dan and excitedly greeted him. Wes gave him a bear hug, his face bursting with emotion. "Dan, we heard the news from the officers and this is unbelievable! We're so relieved that she survived!" Gina ran into Dan's arms and they briefly embraced. She tearfully exclaimed, "You need to get going! We'll take our car and follow you to the hospital."

Dan grabbed his down jacket and wool gloves hanging on the front closet door. Hurrying outside they met the sheriff and deputy, and as Dan rushed past them, he waved and replied, "Later, sheriff. Got to run!" Hopping aboard, the ambulance sped off toward the hospital with its siren blaring and a cavalcade of squad cars in close pursuit.

CHAPTER 3
(Sunday, February 21, 2016)

Approaching Archer Memorial Hospital, nursing and medical staff hurried out to greet them. They rushed Annie and Dan into the emergency room and escorted Gina and Wes to the waiting room. Dan spent some time standing next to Annie's bed, holding her hand and trying to reassure her she would be okay. Looking at her tiny, battered body he had his doubts, yet he knew he needed to stay hopeful for her sake.

Beyond exhaustion, Dan fielded questions now being fired at him by the nurses, doctors and police officers who greeted him in the ER. He lost track of how many times he repeated his grim story to them as they stared at him in disbelief. He nervously glanced over his shoulder at Annie as she lie in bed with closed eyes amidst a complex maze of tubes and wires attached to her small body. She was surrounded by doctors and nurses, had an IV in her arm and a tube in her mouth to help her breathe. She also had wires attached to her chest, monitoring her vital signs and heart rhythm. Dan wanted nothing more than to hold her in his arms and have her be awake when he told her how much he loved her.

Dr. Richard Wilson, one of the ER doctors, approached and introduced himself to Dan. "Mr. Stevens, I'm Dr. Wilson, the primary doctor in charge of your daughter's care. We need to get her into surgery right now, as her injuries are very serious. May we have your consent?" He handed Dan a surgical consent form to sign.

"Most certainly, Dr. Wilson. Can you please tell me the nature of her injuries and what surgery will be performed?"

"Your daughter has several chest and abdominal wounds and is having difficulty breathing. That's why she has the breathing machine. I believe she has a collapsed lung and blood in her chest wall, so she needs to have a chest tube inserted to remove the blood and re-inflate her lung," he explained. "We'll also need to examine her abdomen and make sure she's not bleeding internally in that area."

"I understand," Dan replied. "Do you know how long she'll be in surgery?"

"Most likely for several hours." Dr. Wilson and Dan exchanged glances as Dan handed back the signed consent form.

"Dr. Wilson, please… please save Annie's life! She's the only family I have left, other than my sister and mother," Dan heavily sighed. The ordeal he underwent was obvious on his haggard-looking face and in his limp body posture.

"Mr. Stevens, I will do my best. I'll check with the ICU nurses on a room on the same floor, so you can catch some sleep. I'll keep you posted on her progress." Dr. Wilson shook hands with Dan and hurried down the hall toward the elevator.

Dan watched Dr. Wilson get into the elevator, then he headed toward the waiting room. Entering the room, he noticed Gina and Wes were the only people waiting. They looked at him as he entered and rushed to greet him. Quickly glancing at his watch, he noticed it was 3:45 a.m.

"Dan, how is she?" Gina inquired. Wes stood next to her and Dan noticed he was trying to hide a yawn.

"She's in surgery now. Dr. Wilson said it will be at least several hours before we hear any news. He told me she has a collapsed lung with blood in her chest and some abdominal wounds as well."

"Was she awake when you were with her?" Wes asked.

"No, she was unconscious…" Dan's voice trailed off to barely a whisper. Staring at Wes and Gina in front of him he realized how much he had put them through, and although glad for their support and companionship, he now wanted to try to get some sleep. "Hey, why don't you guys go home to rest and I'll stay here with Annie. I'll contact you when I hear some news."

Gina hugged Dan and replied, "You need to get some sleep as well!" She stared at him with concern. "You sure you'll be alright without us sticking around?"

"Yeah, Dr. Wilson said he'll notify the nurses about a place for me to sleep in Annie's room, so I can be with her."

"Dan, you know you always have a place to stay with us," Gina offered. Dan shook his head.

"I know you guys have your own lives and have to work. I need to be with Annie."

Gina thought for a moment and reaching into her purse,

she pulled out a key. "Here's the key to our cabin. If you need some alone time, you can stay there for as long as you need." Dan took the key and thanked her.

Wes slipped his arm around Dan's right shoulder. He winced when Wes's hand touched the knife wound.

"You know where to find us if you need us." Wes studied Dan's face for a moment and noticed his torn, blood-stained t-shirt. "Better have that shoulder checked." Dan nodded and watched them leave. He then headed down the hall toward the nurses' station.

When he reached the station, a nurse sitting behind the desk recognized and greeted him. "You're Annie Stevens' father, right?" Dan nodded. Noticing he was holding his right shoulder, she asked if he was okay.

"Yeah, I'm just wondering if you know where Annie will be taken after her surgery?" The nurse got up and walked over to Dan.

"She will be taken upstairs to the ICU. They are expecting you." Casually glancing at his blood-stained shirt, she declared, "I think we had better look at that shoulder." Motioning him toward an open exam room, he sat down in a chair as the nurse examined his wound. Informing him he would need sutures to close the wound, she left the room to find a doctor. While waiting for the doctor, he dozed. In a few minutes, he was awakened by the doctor and nurse as they came into the exam room.

The doctor shook Dan's hand. He introduced himself as Dr. McCarthy and went to work suturing Dan's shoulder wound. "This looks fairly deep, so you're lucky it didn't extend into your rotator cuff." After he finished the procedure, he wished Dan good luck with Annie and left the room. The nurse applied a dressing and gave Dan wound care instructions and dressing supplies. Thanking her, he walked down the hall to the elevator and took it up to the 3rd floor where the ICU was located.

Dan approached the nurses' station and asked one nurse if there was any report on his daughter. Shaking her head, she replied, "Nothing as yet, as she's still in surgery. We'll let you know as soon as we hear from the doctor." She pointed toward the staff lounge informing him he was welcome to make himself comfortable there.

Dan walked down the hall and entered the lounge. Glancing around the room, he noticed a few tables and chairs, a small kitchen area and a black leather couch located in front of a window. Dragging his weary body toward the couch, he slumped down onto it. He closed his tired eyes and his mind replayed the day's events. Images of him going upstairs and finding Gina's note on her bed came to mind. Reaching in his pocket, he found her note and read it again.

He pictured his older sister consoling him when he got into fights with a few classmates when they were kids in the school playground. When he came home with bruises and a black eye, she hugged him and told him his "war wounds," as she called them, gave him "character." He smiled as he remembered Gina playing nanny when Annie and Stephanie were babies. *At least I still have her,* he thought, and felt relieved that she had left the house before the murders occurred. Folding the note, he placed it back in his pocket and soon fell into an exhausted slumber.

Peering into his attacker's sinister eyes, he was seized

with a strange sense of recognition, yet a stronger, more urgent need arose to defend himself from the knife held mere inches from his throat. Swinging his arms and legs, he lashed out at the attacker with renewed fury.

Someone was now trying to restrain him. Awakening from his nightmare, he was lying on the floor of the staff lounge with two security guards holding him down.

"What the hell?" he bellowed still in a daze from the nightmare, his body sweating profusely. One of the guards was now patting his good shoulder.

"It's okay, Mr. Stevens. You were having a bad dream, that's all."

After a few moments, as he allowed himself to calm down, the guards helped him to his feet and he sat down on the couch. Glancing at his watch, he saw it was 7 a.m. and realized he had only slept for an hour. He nervously scanned the room and noticed the same nurse who he spoke to at the nurses' station walked toward him.

"Mr. Stevens, Annie is now in recovery and you can see her for a few minutes."

"How is she doing?" he urgently asked.

"She's asleep, yet stable. Dr. Wilson will be in shortly to talk with you."

Dan followed the nurse into the recovery room and rushed to his daughter's bedside. Observing Annie, he was overcome with emotion. He reached for her tiny hand and held it lovingly in his own hand. Bending over her bed, he kissed her forehead and whispered, "It's going to be alright, sweetheart. Daddy's here with you. You're going to be alright."

He marveled at how tiny Annie appeared swathed in a

maze of bandages, tubes, and wires amidst a sea of machinery towering above her. Still in a state of shock and exhaustion from the day's events, he listened to the asynchronous rhythms of the respirator, cardiac monitor, and IV and suction pumps surrounding her bed.

She's had a rough go of it. Dan's thoughts were interrupted when Dr. Wilson walked into the room. Dan turned around to see the doctor still wearing his surgical mask around his neck. "How did the surgery go?" Dan asked approaching the doctor.

"She had some pretty serious stab wounds to her chest and abdomen. Her chest was filled with blood and her lung collapsed, requiring us to insert a chest tube to re-inflate her lung. Luckily, her abdominal wounds weren't as deep and her intestines remained intact. Annie's a fighter like her father," Dr. Wilson smiled and patted Dan's good shoulder reassuringly.

Dan breathed a sigh of relief. "How long will she be in the hospital?"

"She will be here in ICU for perhaps the next week or so until she is able to breathe on her own and we can remove the chest tube and respirator. She will then be transferred to a regular floor for observation and we'll see how it goes from there."

Dan blankly stared at Dr. Wilson with tired eyes and resisted his body's urge to collapse from fatigue.

"What are her chances of leading a normal life after all this?"

"Her recovery might be lengthy considering all the trauma she's been through, yet her chances are good. She has youth and a loving dad on her side." Dr. Wilson paused and gazed at Dan with concern at his haggard appearance. "By the way, have you had any chance to catch some sleep?" Dan shook his head.

"I don't think there's anything more you can do for Annie at present. So, why don't you go back to wherever you're staying to get some rest? You have to think about yourself as well, Mr. Stevens. Do you have a place to stay?"

Remembering the key Gina gave him, he nodded.

"Yes, I have my sister's cabin."

"Do you have a ride?"

"No, I rode the ambulance."

Glancing at his watch, Dr. Wilson replied, "Well, you're in luck. The night shift is getting ready to leave, and I'm sure we can find someone who can drive you to your cabin." Dr. Wilson smiled and extended his hand toward Dan. "Get some rest and we'll stay in touch about Annie."

After thanking Dr. Wilson, Dan turned and walked down the hall toward the lounge. He wearily dropped onto the couch, and gazed out the window at the dawning of a new day.

The hospital security guard dropped him off at Gina's cabin. Opening the door with the key she gave him, he quickly shed his jacket and gloves and threw them on the floor. He dragged himself through the front room, past the small kitchenette and into the bedroom at the back of the cabin. He peeled off his bloodied and sweat-soaked clothing and fell into bed. He closed his eyes and surrendered to exhaustion and a deep and dreamless slumber.

CHAPTER 4
(Wednesday, February 24, 2016)

A few nights later around midnight, George and Susan Adams stood arm in arm at their front room window gazing out at the full moon. Snow was lightly falling and the ground was covered with crystals of ice and snow sparkling in the moon's luminescent glow. It was the end of a nearly perfect day.

After leaving the Marines in 2004, George landed a job as an engineer in Portland, Maine, and then met Susan who also worked at the same company as an administrative secretary. They got married in 2007 and by 2009, the company offered George a better paying engineering position in Lakeland, Maine. Susan was able to find accounting work online that allowed her to work from home.

After serving four years in the Marines along with his fellow marine, Dan Stevens, George wanted to settle into a simpler lifestyle. He and Susan talked about living in the country and eventually found a perfect home. It was a log cabin that needed some work, yet it was affordable. After doing some remodeling of both outside and inside log structures, they settled in and lived a comfortable life in their cabin for the past seven years.

The cabin was 1725 square feet, a two-level log structure that was originally built in the mid-nineties. It had 2 bedrooms and bathrooms, and plenty of windows with breathtaking views of Mount Katahdin in the distance, the highest peak in the state of Maine. George and Susan had recently remodeled the front room. They had added on a few more square feet to the front room to create more space and openness. They had also added cathedral ceilings and a stone fireplace/chimney to add a homey touch to the rustic atmosphere.

Earlier that evening, they returned from a three-hour snowshoe trek through the densely wooded forest surrounding their log cabin. As they stood by the bay window in their front room, they shared conversation about the day and their lives together.

"I love this place, George. I'm glad we moved away from the city. I loved seeing the mama moose and her baby again today."

"Yes, me too. Perhaps you are fond of mama and her brood because you are also in a family way," George smiled and gently patted her pregnant belly.

"In another month, little Lynette will make her appearance. I can't wait," Susan declared.

George stared intently at Susan, admiring her long, dark brown hair and eyes of the same color. "Are you sure you're ready? When she comes, that means we won't have much time, if any, for snowshoeing, hikes, or us."

"I'm well aware of that, George. We've discussed this before. Since we moved here, we've enjoyed ourselves without being tied down with children. Now I really feel ready to be a mom." Smiling, Susan gazed lovingly up at George and flung her arms around his neck. They had known each other for twelve years. She recalled his tall, muscular build, grey-green eyes, and sandy brown hair attracted her when they first met. "Besides, we need a bit more noise around here," she chuckled.

"Yeah, you're right. It has been rather quiet around here." They embraced and kissed for a while. "Hey, do you want to watch the late show for a bit before hitting the sack?" George asked.

Susan walked over to the brown corduroy sofa close to the window where they were standing. She yawned and slumped down into the soft mauve pillows on the sofa. "I'm a bit tired, but, yes, we can watch for a while."

George sat next to her on the sofa, and picked up the remote and turned on the TV. Channel surfing, he tried to find their favorite late night show, yet paused when the late night news came on.

"…we are still looking for the assailant who attacked Dan Stevens, killing his wife, Peggy, and their daughter, Stephanie, in their home in Archer three nights ago. His older daughter, Annie, is still in critical condition at Archer Memorial Hospital. Sheriff Anderson is asking for anyone with information to please contact the Archer Sheriff's Office."

George yelled out and felt Susan suddenly grab his hand with a force he never previously felt from her. "Oh, my God, George!" she gasped.

"I need to call Dan." Trying to remain as calm as possible, he dialed Dan's number. The phone rang several times before he heard Dan's voice on his message machine.

George realized it was late and thought that Dan was probably asleep. He left a message for Dan to call him as soon as possible. After leaving the message, he hugged and tried to console Susan who was now sobbing. *Who would do such a thing?* His mind and heart were racing, and he wondered if his life would ever be the same again.

The man known as Silas Samuels drove his fifth generation 2010 red Chevy Camaro into the parking lot of a Super 6 Motel about a half hour's drive from Lakeland, Maine. He got out of the car carrying a small black valise and walked into the motel lobby. He approached the front desk and brushed some snow off his black trench coat. The clerk greeted him. "Good evening, sir. May I help you?"

"Yes, I'd like a room," the man replied.

"Very good, sir. I do still have a few rooms available. Will this just be for yourself?"

The man nodded.

"I do have one last room with a queen-size bed. It's a smoking room. Will that be okay?"

"Yes."

"…and your name, sir?"

"Wilbur Williams."

"Mr. Williams, how long will you be staying?"

"Just for the night."

"May I see your ID, sir?" The man showed his fake ID and paid for his room. The clerk held his ID a bit longer and studied the picture for a few moments. "So, you're from Vermont, I see. That's a fairly long drive from here."

The man shifted his feet and thought for a moment. "It's an urgent family situation."

"I see…" The clerk paused for another moment and met the man's gaze directly. "Sir, you're all set. Your room is 224 on the second floor at the end of the hall on your left, and here's the key. Have a good night."

"Same to you." The man took the key in his gloved hand and walked to the elevator. After riding up to the second floor, he turned left and headed down the hall to his room. Entering the room, he took off his trench coat and gloves and threw them on a nearby chair.

Sitting on the bed, he lit a cigarette, opened his valise and pulled out a photo of George Adams wearing his Marine combat uniform. Blowing smoke from his nostrils and mouth, he studied the photo for a few moments.

Memories from fifteen years prior filled his ravaged mind. As he ran through a heavily wooded area surrounding the small nearby town in Afghanistan, the sound of machine gunfire ripped through the air. He and one of his marine comrades, Corporal Ryan Morris, were shooting at Taliban soldiers pursuing them. A bomb exploded nearby and suddenly Morris fell to the ground with blood streaming from his head. He also landed on the ground a few feet away from Morris, who yelled something at him. He vividly heard in his mind's eye Morris calling him by his last name, as did his other squadron mates.

"I'm hit, Samuels! Get some help!"

Crawling over to where his comrade lay, he applied pressure with his hand over Morris' gaping head wound. He blankly stared at Morris and saw him lying motionless. He tried to rouse Morris when Samuels realized he was unconscious.

Scanning the area for some sight of his squadron mates, all he could see were advancing Taliban soldiers. After several minutes of doing chest compressions, he still couldn't feel any pulse. He couldn't bear the sight of his comrade dying right in front of him. Frantically searching the area for some form of shelter, he observed a bomb-shattered building nearby still smoldering from the previous explosion. He quickly stood and dragged Morris behind the structure.

After another explosion, Samuels pressed his hands to his ears to try to stop the ringing sound. Fearing for his own life, he started running away from the combat area. After running for a few minutes, he heard someone yell his name and looking behind him, he saw George and Sergeant Griffin sprinting after him. "Samuels, you son of a bitch! Stop, you coward!" George soon caught up with him, grabbed him by the collar of his uniform and threw him to the ground. "Are you deserting your squadron? You can't leave! We're in the midst of combat and you're running away?" George furiously yelled.

Samuels pointed toward the wreckage where Morris lie, and yelled back at George. "Morris is hurt…" The sound of gunfire was again surrounding them.

George dove to the ground right next to him, rolled on his back and fired his M4 carbine in the direction of the advancing Taliban soldiers. Griffin also fired his weapon at the soldiers, and ran toward the wreckage where Morris was hidden.

Samuels remembered squinting his eyes in the fast falling dusk and noticed ten to fifteen enemy soldiers were approaching and surrounding them. In a panic, he stood and tried to flee, but felt a sharp tug on his pant leg causing him to fall again on the ground face first. Once again the sound of rapid machine gunfire was heard. George was whispering to him now as he scanned the area. "Samuels!" He pointed to the burned out remnants of what used to be a building. "Over there! On the count of three, let's go! One… two… three!"

In a flash, George and Samuels sprinted toward the structure amidst a furious spray of gunfire. The clamor of ammunition pinging off the buildings and nearby trees surrounding them was deafening as they sprinted toward the hovel. Reaching shelter at last, George flung his body through the doorway and landed with a thud on the ground in the structure. Peering out, George watched as Samuels ran toward him, clutching his bloody left leg and howling in pain. Once again he fell to the ground.

In an instant, George dashed from the structure and grabbed Samuels by his good leg and dragged him into the enclosure. Crouching down behind it, George loaded the M203 single shot grenade launcher and fired it directly into the approaching battalion of Taliban soldiers. The explosion shook the ground, sent a blast of flames through the forest and caused chaos amongst the flank of soldiers. Most fled through the forest with the remaining soldiers lying bleeding on the ground or running wildly in panic-stricken circles with clothes and skin ablaze.

George, ever watchful of approaching enemies, turned to face Samuels rolling around on the ground, holding his bloody leg and moaning in pain. Looking up at George, Samuels yelled, "Let me die! Save yourself!"

"Shut up, Samuels! You're not gonna die on my watch! And you better have a good story to tell the Master Sergeant." He grabbed a large twig from the ground, pulled a handkerchief from his pocket and fashioned a tourniquet around Samuels' leg.

Suddenly, the sound of leaves crunching behind him caused him to quickly stand and turn around as he grabbed for his M9 Beretta. George stared into the dirt-caked faces of squad mates Master Sergeant Nielson, and Corporal Stevens pointing their rifles at them.

Master Sergeant Nielson silently breathed a sigh of relief as he recognized his squad mates. "So, what's the story here, Sergeant? Where did you guys go?" he asked lowering his rifle. Stevens also lowered his rifle on a signal from Nielson.

"Samuels here started freaking out and I chased him down and tried to bring him back to the squad, yet as you can see, he almost got himself and the rest of us killed, sir," George replied staring straight ahead at the Master Sergeant. Nielson nodded and glanced down at Samuels lying on the ground.

"Sir, I was with Morris when he was wounded. I tried to tell him Morris was hurt when we were in the midst of heavy gunfire," Samuels tried to explain.

"Let's get him up and us out of here. I'll try to find Morris," he ordered. In a flash, Nielson ran outside the structure and disappeared into the forest. George and Dan helped Samuels stand up on his right leg. They ran from the hovel with Samuels supported between them, and continued running until they reached their camp.

Samuels was taken to a nearby MASH unit where he

underwent surgery to remove the bullet from his leg. Several military police stood guard next to his bed. He wanted to ask them why they were there, yet was too groggy from the anesthesia to talk and fell back asleep.

A few hours later, he awoke and seeing the MP's still standing guard by his bed, he called out to them. "Why are you guys here?"

"Orders from the top," was the reply from one of his guards.

Scanning the room, Samuels noticed Master Sergeant Nielson approaching his bed. Nielson spoke a few words to the MP's and came over to the side of the bed. They exchanged glances and Samuels saluted him and was the first to speak. "Sir, thanks for your visit."

"At ease, Samuels. You won't be thanking me, I can assure you. I have talked with your squadron mates, Sergeant Griffin and Corporal Stevens, and of course, Sergeant Adams who saved your life. Based on their stories, you're in a lot of trouble." He paused and let out a heavy breath, weighing his next words.

Samuels interrupted his thoughts. "What happened to Morris?"

"Griffin found him and he's also here in the unit. He told Griffin that you were with him when the bomb exploded and he was injured. I also spoke with him. You do have one thing in your favor, that you tried to help him. I just talked with the doctor and he informed me you can be released from this MASH unit within the next few days. You will then be flown to a detention facility in Germany and after your release, you will be flown back to the States to face charges of desertion in a court of law with a possible dishonorable discharge."

Samuels was silent for a moment and deep in thought. *How will I be able to stand trial?* He wondered if it would even be a fair trial?

Averting his gaze down toward his wounded, now throbbing leg, Samuels repositioned his heavily bandaged leg and the throbbing subsided. *This situation doesn't bode well for me*, he thought. He remembered the doctor visiting him after surgery, and vaguely recalled the doctor telling him it would take months and possibly years for his leg to completely heal. *Will I ever be able to walk normally again?*

"Do you have anything to say in your defense?" Nielson interrupted his thoughts.

Samuels directed his gaze back toward Nielson. "As you previously mentioned, I did my best to try to save Morris' life. I'm innocent until proven guilty and I have the right to retain a lawyer, sir."

"Yes, one will either be assigned or you can retain legal representation of your choice at your expense."

"Okay…good to know."

"Get some rest. I'll keep you informed as to further proceedings." Samuels nodded and watched Nielson hurry out of the unit.

When he was finally able to get out of bed, a nurse helped him into a wheelchair. He asked her where Morris' room was, and paid Morris a visit. During the conversation they had, Morris mentioned having a talk with the Master Sergeant, and he thanked Samuels for saving his life. Morris even refused to testify against him in court for this reason.

He recalled the court scene of the remaining squadron

mates reporting their allegations against him, and the ensuing two year prison sentence and dishonorable discharge.

"Assholes ratted on me," Samuels said aloud, pounding his fist on the nightstand next to the bed. He felt a familiar rage welling up inside him as he took another drag on his cigarette. Blowing smoke at the photo of George, he shredded it and threw the pieces into the wastebasket. "You, my comrade, will regret it."

Reaching into his valise, he pulled out a dagger and sharpening tool and started to sharpen the dagger. Finally, satisfied the weapon was ready for action, he replaced it and the tool back in the valise and closed the lid. He grabbed his coat, gloves, and valise and hurried outside to his Camaro. A biting wind and blinding snowstorm greeted him as he got in, slammed the door in frustration, and started driving toward Lakeland.

George pulled himself away from Susan after they made love and rolled over on his side. He gazed lovingly at her lying next to him in bed and brushed a strand of brown hair away from her eyes. "I love you," he whispered and smiled.

Susan smiled and sleepily yawned. "I love you, too. Sorry, but I'm pretty tired."

"You've had a busy day. Sleep tight, baby." He watched her eyes close and soon heard her lightly snore. He rolled over on his back and stared at the ceiling, wide awake for a while. He tried to shake an uneasiness that suddenly overcame him.

Rising slowly from their bed so as not to wake Susan, he turned out the bedroom light and headed to the shower as per his nightly routine. He lingered there longer than usual, enjoying the sensation of warm water spraying down on him, soothing away all his tension. He thought about Dan and his family and muttered a silent prayer.

After a long, slow drive through the snowstorm, Samuels finally reached the Adams' house and parked out of sight behind some trees and bushes with his lights turned off. Glancing at the house through the windshield, he noticed the house was dark except for a dim light that shined through an upstairs bathroom window.

Checking his cell, he saw it was 2:15 a.m. and thought it strange that someone was still awake at that time. He decided to wait in the car where it was warm until the light went out. He would then make his move.

Images of scenes from his court-martial fifteen years prior flashed before him as though they had occurred the previous day. He could almost hear the testimonies of his squad mates, accusing him of desertion. George's face appeared in mid-air right before his eyes, as he told his story of chasing Samuels and throwing him to the ground. Suddenly, the voice switched to that of the judge declaring him guilty as charged and imposing a two year prison sentence.

Samuels closed his eyes and tried to shut out the flashbacks, yet they were relentless. Pounding his fist down on the dashboard, he turned his attention to the upstairs bedroom window and saw it was now dark.

He turned off the heat in the Camaro and slowly opened the door. A gust of frigid wind and spindrift blew directly into his face. The snow was still steadily falling as he shielded his face with his arm and made his way with penlight in hand to the front door of George's house. Glancing at his cellphone, he noticed it was now almost 3 a.m.

Samuels grabbed the doorknob with his gloved hand and discovered the door was locked. Walking toward the back of the house, he approached one ground floor window and broke the glass with the dagger's hilt.

George was stepping out of the shower and stopped dead in his tracks. *What was that noise?* he wondered. *It sounded like broken glass, or perhaps someone was knocking at the front door.* Grabbing for a towel next to the shower, he quickly dried himself off and pulled on his pants. Once again, he paused and listened for any further noises, but heard only silence.

Samuels hurried upstairs and crept past the closed bathroom door down the hall and toward the master bedroom.

Slowly opening the bathroom door, a sliver of light from the bathroom nightlight dimly silhouetted the darkened hallway. George hurried out of the bathroom and walked down the hallway to the staircase leading downstairs. The faint light from the nightlight guided him. As George made his way downstairs, Samuels hid himself against a darkened corner of the hallway near the master bedroom.

Reaching the front room, George turned on a small lamp sitting on the table near the windows closest to the front door. Glancing at the windows, he saw they were intact.

He peered through the front door peephole and saw no one there. Turning around, he hurried toward the windows that were on the other side of the room where he felt a rush of cold air coming from one of the windows. Glancing down, he noticed pieces of broken glass lying on the windowsill, with the window open and the curtains blowing wildly in the breeze. Seized with fear he wondered, *who would be breaking into the house at this time of night?*

Remembering the news about the attacker, he felt his heart pounding in his chest. He knew that someone was in the house and he raced back upstairs taking two stairs at a time.

Approaching the bedroom, he heard a muffled scream. He flung open the bedroom door just in time to see a man straddling Susan, holding one hand over her mouth and the other brandishing a bloody knife.

George sprinted inside the room, flung his body directly at the attacker and knocked him to the floor. The attacker landed with a thud on his back with George sprawled on top of him. With the knife still held tight in his hand, the attacker swung his knife and stabbed George in the back. George yelled in pain and furiously grabbed behind him trying to extricate the knife. The attacker already had his hand on the knife, pulled it from George's back and held his hand above George ready to plunge it again into his back. George grabbed the attacker's arm in mid-air and wrestled the knife out of his grasp. The knife fell to the floor a mere few feet away from them.

Breathing out heavily, George gathered all his remaining strength and clutched his hand around the attacker's neck in a strangle hold. With his other hand, he tried to pull the mask off the attacker's face. The attacker grabbed George's hand and pushed it away from his face. George heard gurgling noises coming from inside the mask and he clamped his hand down harder on the attacker's windpipe. He noticed the attacker's arms fell limply back to the floor and he was now lying motionless. Releasing his death grip on the man's neck, he rolled off the man and wearily peered up at Susan lying in a crumpled heap on the bed.

George tried to get up off the floor when suddenly the attacker reached for the knife and sprang back into action. Wielding his knife, the attacker plunged it into George's thigh and with his other hand pulled him back down on the floor. George, now operating on adrenaline, wrestled the knife out of the attacker's hand and flung it across the room out of reach. He knew his next move needed to be on target and might be his last. Swinging his good leg up, he kicked at the attacker's face which sent the man sprawling on the floor. As George tried again to stand, the man picked himself up and ran at George, knocking him over on his side.

Suddenly, another figure appeared from the direction of the bed, and before George knew what was happening, heard a vase shattering on the floor next to him. Staring blankly up at Susan, he saw that she was standing over him holding one hand over her bleeding, protruding belly while her other hand held remnants of the shattered vase.

Reaching for his bleeding head, the attacker released his grip on George, got up off the floor and pushed Susan to the floor. Picking up the knife, he ran from the room down the hall to the stairs and outside into the frigid early morning air.

Bleeding heavily from his thigh and back wounds, George wearily dragged his body across the floor to where Susan lay in a motionless heap next to their bed. Finally reaching her, he rolled her over on her back and gently shook her shoulders.

"Baby, are you alright?" When she didn't reply, George felt her neck for a pulse and found it was very weak. He immediately started chest compressions and continued for five minutes until he knew her pulse was stronger, yet she remained motionless with her eyes closed. He noticed she was barely breathing and her nightgown was soaked with blood.

"Baby, please stay with me!" he begged. Reaching in his pants pocket for his phone, he called 911, and suddenly feeling faint, he succumbed to the surrounding blackness.

CHAPTER 5
(Thursday, February 25, 2016)

Gasping for air, Dan sat bolt upright and leaned his back against a nearby tree. Pulling his coat closer around his body, he tried to slow his breath and racing heart as the visions slowly started to fade from his memory. Gazing up at the slivers of moonlight filtering through the surrounding dense forest, he muttered a prayer that God would spare him the torment of repeatedly reliving the nightmare.

Dan blew out an extended breath into the chilly night air and glanced around at the endless forest and pervasive darkness that gave him momentary solace. For the past few days since Annie was hospitalized and lying in a coma fighting for her life, Dan had been spending his nights walking around the forest behind Gina's cabin where he now lived. The forest provided a safe, solitary space for him to be alone and sort out his thoughts.

Realizing it was well after midnight, he decided to head back to the cabin. After the senseless slaying of his wife and daughter, Gina told him he could stay in the cabin until he was able to return to his house. He made a few feeble attempts to go back there to retrieve some clothing and personal belongings, yet it was too painful to stay. Dan walked toward the path leading out of the forest and began his thirty minute walk back to the solitude of his cabin.

Approaching the cabin, Dan stood outside the front door noticing its features and architecture. It was a light brown log cabin tucked away in a white pine forest overlooking a rushing mountain stream. He stared intently at its structure and remembered his dad telling him that he built the cabin in 1973. His dad was an architect and owned his own business, Stevens Architecture, for several years before Dan was born. Dan inherited the business after his dad's passing five years ago. He marveled at his dad's artistic placement of every log and suddenly missed his presence.

Dan smiled at the thought of his mother, and recalled that she worked as dad's secretary until his passing. *She was just as devastated,* he thought. *I need to call her later when I get a chance.*

Dan unlocked the door and entered the cabin. He picked up a few pieces of wood from the wood bin and soon got a fire started in the fireplace. He removed his coat and gloves and threw them on the couch. He warmed his hands over the flickering flames.

Staring into the fire, he reminisced about Peggy. He remembered when the two of them would sit on the couch next to the fireplace holding hands and recounting the day's events.

He could almost smell her perfume and feel the gentle touch of her hand against his skin. He could feel her presence even now only a few days after her untimely death, her blue eyes meeting his loving gaze, the feel of her honey blonde hair brushing against his face as they passionately kissed. *God, how I miss her,* he thought.

He recalled how they made love in front of the fireplace and the vivid memories brought tears of longing to his eyes. *If I ever catch that son of a bitch...* In a fit of rage, he pounded his fist down upon the mantelpiece. Walking to the couch, he sat and held his head in his hands and shed bitter tears of anger and grief.

He glanced up at the clock on the wall above the fireplace and noticed it was 2 a.m. Feeling a wave of exhaustion overcome him, he laid down on the couch and soon fell into a fitful sleep. After a time, he started dreaming and was once again drawn back to the previous night when his Peggy and Stephanie were murdered by an intruder. *There they are again!* The visions of him running into his bedroom in a state of shock and grief-stricken over the murders of his wife and daughter. Visions of him discovering Peggy's stabbed and blood-stained body lying on the floor face down next to the open window. Visions of a man of medium height and build dressed in a black trench coat, mask and gloves, brandishing a knife and trying to escape through the open window.

Dan awakened soaked with sweat, and with a yell he sprang to an upright position on the couch. Glancing at the clock, he noticed it was now close to 7 a.m. and realized he had only been asleep for a few hours. He got up from the couch and still groggy from his short nap, headed toward the bathroom.

He walked over to the sink, turned on the faucet and splashed cold water on his face. Grabbing his towel, he dried his face and hands. With the memory of his nightmarish visions still fresh in his mind, he paused for a moment, staring at his haggard, unshaven reflection in the mirror above the sink. So much had happened within the past five days, he could barely process it all.

Dan walked back into the front room, sat down on the couch and stared into space. Listening to the sound of absolute silence, at one time a welcome ambience, now disturbed him. He got up and turned on the TV just to hear another human voice. It came in the form of the morning news reporter recounting the day's events. At first, he listened to the weather report. "It looks like more snow is due for the Archer area, with an additional four to five inches for the mountains…"

Dan felt an overwhelming fatigue engulf his body so he laid back down on the couch. Starting to doze again, the news reporter's voice interrupted his brief nap.

"Breaking news… a pregnant woman was viciously attacked by an intruder who broke into her home last night in Lakeland, Maine. Both Susan and her husband, George Adams, have been taken to Lakeland Memorial Hospital in serious condition…"

Once again, Dan sat bolt upright staring blankly at the TV screen, not believing what he was hearing. The reporter continued. "One neighbor claimed to have been awakened by the sounds of people fighting and a loud crash coming from the Adams house earlier this morning around 4 a.m. The neighbor claimed he saw a masked man running away from the house holding a knife and driving off in a red Camaro. If anyone has seen this man or has any information on this man's where-abouts, please contact the number on your screen for the Lake-land Police Department or your local authorities."

"Oh my God! Not George and Susan!" Dan yelled at the TV, his thunderous voice resonating throughout the once peaceful silence of the cabin. He got up, reached in his pocket for his cell and with trembling hand dialed Sheriff Anderson's number. The phone rang several times before he heard the sher-iff's familiar gruff, monotone voice.

"Dan, I was expecting your call. I'm assuming you heard about the attack on the couple up in Lakeland."

"Sheriff, I'm thinking there's got to be a connection. The mask, the knife…" he paused for a moment to collect his scattered thoughts. There was something familiar about the man, yet his sleep-deprived brain couldn't make the connec-tion. "I know George and his wife, Susan. George was one of five in my squad when I served in the Marines. Do you have any further news on their condition or the guy who attacked them?"

Sheriff Anderson cleared his throat. "I have some de-tails I'd like to talk about with you. I've called in a detective who has more experience in dealing with serial killers and I'd like you to meet her. Can you come down to the station?"

"Be there as soon as I can." Dan disconnected the call and shoved his cell back in his shirt pocket. As he reached for his coat laying on the couch and headed toward the door, his cell phone rang. The voice on the other end belonged to his sis-ter Gina, and he was immediately bombarded with her numer-ous questions.

"Dan, I've been so worried about you. I've left a few

messages and didn't hear from you. Are you okay? Have you seen the news? Were you able to get any rest? Any word yet on Annie?"

"Hey, sis. Yes, I'm okay. I've seen the news and no updates on Annie. She is still in critical condition in ICU. To be honest, I haven't had a moment to breathe since this whole thing went down." He stared down at the floor in a trance-like state, trying to make sense of the horrific events that occurred only five days ago.

"I'm coming over, brother. It sounds like you need some company right now and…" Remembering his conversation with the sheriff, he interrupted Gina.

"Gina, now's not a good time. I'm heading over to the station to talk with Sheriff Anderson and some special detective he called in on the case. So, you've seen the news about the guy attacking George and Susan?"

"YES! Oh my God, Dan, wasn't George one of your squad mates? I can't even imagine what kind of maniac is behind all this!" Gina's voice was now in the upper registers and filled with emotion.

"Can I call you back later? We'll talk more when I know more."

"Dan, I know you're busy and have a lot on your mind, but I just wanted to tell you I will take care of the funeral arrangements. That's one more thing you don't have to worry about. I'm working late tonight and won't get home until seven or eight, but I'll be expecting your call… and good luck!"

Dan thanked her and clicked off his cell. He grabbed his jacket and hurried out the door, forgetting his gloves still laying on the couch. He ran to his 2014 Blue Mustang GT and raced off to his meeting, burning rubber all the way.

While Dan drove to the sheriff's office, he checked his phone and noticed a few messages were from his mother. He listened to them, and heard her worried voice conveying her deepest condolences and concern about her unanswered messages. She also asked about funeral arrangements, and informed him of her imminent travel plans to Archer.

Dan looked forward to seeing her and was relieved that Gina offered to help with final arrangements. With all the horrific events of the past few days, he hadn't had a chance to breathe, much less decide on a final resting place for his beloved wife and daughter. He was always the one in control, yet now had to rely on his remaining family to help him deal with a situation that was out of his control.

CHAPTER 6
(Thursday, February 25, 2016) 10 p.m.

Trace Malone sat alone at the bar inside The High Five, a local bar and grill, and gulped down the last of her gin and tonic. Turning her barstool toward the bar, she focused her attention on the TV. The 10 p.m. news was blaring its report on another serial killer on the loose. It had been another long and stressful day of trying to solve cases and track down criminals, so that was the last thing she needed to hear. She usually closed her eyes in an attempt to shut out the world from her mind, and focused on her breathing, a meditation technique she had learned from a yoga class, yet this broadcast caught her attention. "… this attack was on another former Marine. George Adams and his pregnant wife, Susan…"

Gently brushing a strand of her shoulder length strawberry blonde hair away from her eyes, she breathed out a long sigh, trying to forget the day's events. Despite her best efforts, scenes from the day replayed in her mind.

She recalled sitting at the desk in her office earlier that morning in Waterton, Vermont. Sheriff Anderson called and told her about the killer who murdered an ex-Marine's wife and daughter, and attacked another ex-Marine and his wife.

She had worked together with the sheriff in the past on a few cases, and they had a bit of history between them. They dated for a while, yet when he asked her to move to Archer so they could live closer, she declined his offer. She much preferred the hustle and bustle of big city life and didn't want to be the main topic of small town gossip. Besides, she also found out through the grapevine that the sheriff was already married. However, after he asked her to team up with their department to apprehend this killer, she hesitantly accepted. During the two hour drive to Archer to meet with him, she firmly decided that this visit to Archer would be her last.

Arriving at the sheriff's office, he intently watched her as she walked toward him, standing up from where he sat behind his desk. Extending his hand and gazing directly into her eyes, he greeted her. "Trace, good to see you again. Thanks for agreeing to help us out on this case."

"My pleasure, Sheriff," she smiled at him as they shook hands. Diverting her gaze, she glanced around the sheriff's office and nodded at Deputy Warner who was sitting at his desk a few feet away from where she and the sheriff stood. Joe Warner also stood up from his desk and walked over to them. They exchanged greetings and stood together in awkward silence for a few moments. Trace broke the silence. "So... what information, if any, do you have on this killer?"

Sheriff Anderson was the first to speak. "Well, from our

investigation, it's apparent that this guy has some connection or gripe with the Marines. The jury is still out on that one."

Trace pondered his comment for a few moments.

"There has to be a correlation. Suppose this guy was a former Marine himself, or an angry son of a father who served in the Marines. Any fingerprints found at either of the two crime scenes?"

The sheriff and deputy shook their heads in unison. It was the deputy who spoke this time. "No fingerprints, but we do have the murder weapon from the first murder scene. This guy was in a big hurry and left his knife laying on the floor."

"I'll swing by the coroner's department and examine the weapon. Any autopsy reports on Dan's wife and daughter yet?"

Sheriff Anderson reached behind him for a brown manila folder laying on his desk and handed it to Trace. "These are only preliminary findings at the scene so that's all I have right now." Before she could open the folder, she noticed a man had walked into the office and had approached them.

Sheriff Anderson greeted the man and introduced him to Trace. "Dan, this is Trace Malone, the detective who will be working with you." She smiled as she turned to face Dan and shake his hand. "It's a pleasure to meet you, Dan." She recalled his six foot frame towering over her petite five-four. "I just want to offer my deepest condolences to you for your wife and daughter."

"Thanks, Trace, for your kind sentiments and for taking this case." She recalled his tired eyes and deep voice laden with sadness and solemn facial expression. Their eyes met and held each other's gaze for a few moments.

Dan broke the silence. "Is Trace your real name?"

She smiled. "Short for Traci. It's a nickname that stuck since my academy days."

Sheriff Anderson changed the subject. "Dan, any news on Annie?"

Dan shifted his gaze to the sheriff and in a monotone voice replied, "Still in the hospital in a coma and still on life support." The sheriff patted Dan's good shoulder. He expressed his sincere wishes for Annie's recovery and suggested they continue the conversation in the interrogation room. He started walking down the hall toward the room when Trace called out to him. "Thanks, Sheriff. I can take it from here."

The sheriff walked back to where they stood and turned to Dan. "If you'll excuse us, I need to talk to the detective for a few minutes." Dan nodded and walked a short distance down the hall. Taking Trace by the arm the sheriff leaned toward her ear and whispered, "How about a drink at Luigi's tonight?"

Trace looked directly into his eyes and with an icy tone in her voice replied, "It's over, Sheriff. I think you should go home tonight to your wife. Am I making myself clear?"

Trace recalled seeing a glimpse of hurt in the sheriff's eyes as he nodded to her when she escorted Dan down the hall to the interrogation room. They had a lengthy conversation about the murders of Dan's wife and daughter. One comment stood out in her mind above all others. He remarked that the killer was somehow very familiar to him, yet he was uncertain as to when or where they had previously met. She reminded herself to check the autopsy reports that the sheriff gave her on Dan's wife and daughter.

"Want any refills, Malone?" The husky male voice of Bill the bartender interrupted her thoughts and brought her back to her seat at the bar.

"No thanks, Bill. I'm good. I should probably get going as I have a busy day again tomorrow."

"Hey, any news on the Stevens case?"

"I'm working on it. Thanks for the drink."

Tapping her fingers softy on the bar, she reached for her purse and slapped a few bills on the counter. *Enough bad news for one day,* she thought.

Tapping his fingers idly on the nightstand next to his bed in the Waterton Motel, Samuels casually smoked a cigarette and watched the 10 p.m. news. Hearing the news, he stamped out his cigarette in the ashtray on the nightstand. The current news report caught his attention as he blew circles of smoke from his last cigarette puff toward the TV.

" . . . the unknown attacker of George and Susan Adams is still at large. Police believe the assailant may be driving a red Camaro according to a witness who saw the vehicle speeding away from the Adams house . . ." The last refrains from the news reporter echoed in his mind.

He ran his hands through his thick, wavy brown hair. Something on his hands felt sticky which caught his attention. Staring at his hands, he noticed they were covered with blood. Getting up from his seat on the bed, he slowly walked over to the sink and washed his hands. He watched the last traces of red liquid circle around and disappear into the drain.

Samuels grinned. "I need to get another car," he reminded himself. Walking back to the bed, he crawled under the covers fully clothed in a black trench coat, white t-shirt, brown pants, and black sneakers. It had been a long seven hour drive from the wilderness of Maine to Waterton, Vermont.

Awakening from a deep sleep around 2 a.m. he was now wide awake. Was he having a nightmare or was it reality? Lying in bed, he turned restlessly from side to side and tried falling back to sleep, yet the images in his mind were haunting and relentless. The images were strangely familiar to him. A small boy was lying naked on his belly on a cold, damp basement floor with a gag in his mouth and his hands tied behind his back. His head throbbed with pain from being hit with something large and hard, and he struggled trying to free his hands from the rope cords that bound them together. A dark shadowy figure stood hovering over him and warned him in a deep masculine voice, "Don't move if you value your life…" The boy was cold, hungry, and shivering with fear. *Why was he hurting me?* he wondered with tears in his eyes.

Samuels tried to make sense of the images that plagued him since childhood, when suddenly a chilling thought occurred to him. Was he that little boy who had never really grown up? His mind was now flooded with more questions than answers. Who was the male figure standing over him? Was that his father or was it someone else?

Shivering in a cold sweat, he flung off the covers, sprang out of bed, and started pacing around the room. After stubbing his toe on one leg of the swivel chair across from his bed, he hobbled in pain toward the nightstand and turned on the light. The clock reflected the time, 2:30 a.m., in big red numerals. He stumbled over to the swivel chair and looked around the room in a daze.

The room smelled of cigarette smoke and was decorated with the usual motel furniture: a small desk by the window, a big screen TV, queen size bed, and swivel chair. *I need a drink,* he thought. *Liquor always helps soothe my jangled nerves and relax me.*

Leaving his second floor room, he walked down the hall to the elevator and rode it down to the lobby. "May I help you sir?" He heard the female voice of the desk clerk as he strode casually by her on his way to the front door leading out to the parking lot. "No, thanks." Heading out the door, a blast of frigid winter air mixed with cold, wet snowflakes slapped his face and woke him up. He got in his Camaro and drove through the snowstorm to a nearby 24 hour convenience store.

Samuels eyed the pretty young blonde-haired girl standing behind the counter. He strolled over to the beer section and picked up a six pack. He walked back to the counter, placed the beer on the counter and smiled back at the blonde.

"Anything else I can get for you, sir?" she asked, smiling sweetly.

"Yes, a pack of Marlboro 100's should do it." He handed her a twenty dollar bill and asked if she was familiar with the neighborhood.

"Yeah, sure. I live in this area," she replied still smiling at him. She handed him his change. Samuels glanced around the store and noticed only a few customers were walking around the aisles.

Returning his gaze back to the girl, he stood for a few moments admiring her long blonde hair, perfect lips, and tall, slender figure. She giggled at his stare and pushed herself away from the counter. "Sir, if there's nothing else you want, I need to get going as it's the end of my shift."

"Of course," Samuels finally spoke. "By the way, do you have a ride? It's pretty nasty outside with all the snow and cold."

"Yeah, I do. My boyfriend is picking me up," she casually replied, still smiling. Noticing her co-worker walking toward the counter to relieve her, she waved to him and started walking toward the break room behind the counter. "Have a good night," she glanced back over her shoulder toward Samuels.

"Oh, okay. Be safe out there. Nice talking to you."

Nodding to the girl's co-worker, Samuels took his beer and cigarettes off the counter and walked out of the store. He got into his Camaro and turned on the car ignition. He enjoyed the blast of heat from the heater and a cold bottle of beer. Sitting in his car for perhaps fifteen minutes or more, he focused on the tall, slender girl now walking toward a car parked on the other side of the lot from where his Camaro was. He watched her reach in her pocket for her keys and get into her car. He wondered where her boyfriend was and stared at her immobile car for a few moments. He heard the sound of her stalled ignition struggling to start. After another failed attempt to start the car, he realized with a certain glee that she wasn't about to go anywhere, anytime soon.

Still sitting in his car, Samuels waited for a few more minutes to see what the girl would do next. He saw her car door open and the girl get out and start walking back toward the convenience store. Samuels got out of his Camaro with the motor still running. He walked toward the store and stood directly in front of her. The girl looked at him with a shocked expression on her face. Samuels was the first to speak. "Dead battery?"

"I…I think so," she stammered, her body shivering in the cold, biting wind blowing snowflakes wildly in the air around them.

"How far do you live? I can give you a ride if you'd like," Samuels offered.

The girl pondered his offer for a few moments, biting her lower lip. "Thanks, but my boyfriend will be picking me up any minute."

He studied her face and noticed her fearful expression. Anger was steadily building up inside him at the realization of her lying to him. *She was so beautiful, he had to have her, to caress her lovely face and body, to hurt her like he was hurt at such a young age…*

"There's my boyfriend now." She broke into a run toward the convenience store, and Samuels noticed a car pulling into the parking lot and heading in her direction. He watched the girl run toward the car. The driver stopped to let the girl get in and the car drove away.

Samuels clenched his fists and ran back to his Camaro. *I can't let them get away! The boyfriend's gotta go!* Flinging open the door, he hurried in and followed behind their car.

As he pulled out of the lot he noticed another car pulling in. In the darkness, he squinted and got a glance at another pretty blonde as their cars passed. Their eyes briefly connected. Samuels stepped on the accelerator and followed the boyfriend's car.

Trace donned her coat, hat, and gloves and hurried out

the door into the bitter cold and dark winter night. She pulled her coat collar closer around her neck. The cold wind wrapped itself around her body, sending shivers up and down her spine. She walked quickly down the snow filled sidewalk and noticed the streets were empty except for parked cars and storefronts with darkened windows.

As she walked, she noticed a lone street lamp across the street and focused her gaze on the light. The lamp emitted an eerie glow silhouetting the heavily falling snowflakes and dimly lit snow covered street. The light cast dark, ominous shadows on car windows as she rushed past. Her car was parked on the next street over from the bar. Trace wished she would have found a closer parking place, yet none were available at the time she arrived at the bar.

A short distance ahead of her on the opposite side of the street, she noticed another bar, Strange Brew. Its gaudy bright red and yellow lights were flickering, beckoning those throw-away social outcasts and blue collar workers seeking shelter from the storm.

Inside the bar, three members of a biker gang, Loose Guns, were gathered, and imbibing far too many pitchers of beer. One of the men turned to look out the window. "Hey, dude, it's dark and it's snowing pretty hard out there. Maybe we should head out." The other biker nodded and grunted in agreement. "Yeah, let's go. We've been here since this afternoon and I think we've already settled a few scores." The bikers got up, threw some loose change onto the table where they sat, knocked over a few chairs, and stumbled toward the door. The bartender scowled at them as they passed by.

They hung outside for a few moments, squinting their

eyes as they peered into the cold, wet snow pelting their black leather jackets. One of the men suddenly caught sight of someone walking across the street and nudged his buddy. "Hey, look at that," he motioned toward the woman walking on the sidewalk across the street.

Trace noticed the three men standing outside looking in her direction and quickened her pace. As she turned the corner and headed toward her car, she heard one of the men call out to her.

"Hey, there, baby doll, I think you dropped something." The sounds of laughter mixed with cigarette smoke filled the air. *Better not engage them in conversation,* she thought. She saw her car about a half block away from where she walked and she wished she were already there.

Hearing footsteps behind her, she had an uneasy feeling that the three men weren't going away anytime soon. One of the men again called out to her. "Where you going in such a hurry there, sweet thing?"

Swinging around to face them, she surveyed her tormenters. *Yeah, like I'm gonna give you the time of day, Sasquatch. Like I really need this bullshit right now.* Rolling her eyes, she reached inside her coat collar to make sure that she still wore the gun and holster vest. *Probably won't need it, yet glad it's there,* she sighed with relief.

The three men were surrounding her in a semicircle near the corner, no more than five feet away from where she stood. The guy to her left had greasy brown shoulder length hair and was tall and lanky, with a cigarette dangling from his mouth. She figured he was the one who called out to her. The guy directly in front of her was short and muscular and held a can of beer to his mouth. *Beer Guy is probably good and sauced,* she mused. The guy standing to her right had his arms folded over his black leather jacket and was short and stout. He wore a goatee and nose ring.

In her bravest and iciest tone, she declared, "You know guys, it's been a long day and I'm not in a very good mood right now, just to let you know."

"Hey, sweetheart, we're just having some fun with you, you know?" The guy with the nose ring sneered at her.

Holding her arms out to her sides in feigned surrender, she declared, "Not tonight, fellas!" Nose Ring was the first to run toward her. Kicking out with her foot, she connected with his face and broke his nose. Clutching his battered and bloody nose, he doubled over in pain. Trace leapt at him, grabbed his head and slammed it into a brick building nearby. He fell over and landed in an unconscious heap on the ground.

Beer Guy dropped his can of beer and had his stout, thick muscular arm around her neck just when she finished with Mr. Nose Ring. Pulling down on his arm with her hand, she managed to slam her other elbow into his gut. He released his grip around her neck and doubled over holding his stomach. Swinging her body around to face him, she landed a fierce karate kick to his knee. Howling in pain, he slumped to the ground and rolled around, cradling his shattered kneecap with his hands.

Trace quickly turned to face Mr. Dangling Cigarette who slowly backed away from her with his hands out in front of him.

"You won't get any trouble from me, ma'am. I'm good." They stared at each other in silence for a few seconds.

Suddenly, he turned and bolted down the street like a smoking, speeding bullet.

She watched him sprint away from her as she sighed and dialed 911. Turning to face the guy writhing on the snowy ground, she said, "Hope you have good insurance, buddy. Would love to stay and chat, but we'll have to take a raincheck." She continued walking down the street toward her car.

Holding her keys, she opened the car door and slid wearily into the driver's seat. Turning the ignition, she noticed the dashboard clock lit up its usual fire red time display: 12:02 a.m. Covering her tired eyes with her hand, she anticipated the long two hour drive back to her office in Waterton and another sleepless night ahead.

Driving back to Waterton was slow and tedious due to the snowstorm. Though there was little traffic on the highways, they were still covered with snow and were slippery. Trace yawned and felt her eyes closing. She knew she was now back in the city, yet still had a distance to drive to get to her office. Sleepily glancing at the dashboard clock, she noticed it was now 3:10 a.m. She decided to pull off Hwy 2 at a local convenience store and get some coffee. The snow was still coming down, yet not as heavily as it was for most of her drive.

She pulled into the convenience store parking lot and noticed a red Camaro drive past her. She caught a quick glimpse of the male driver, yet the lure of pounding down a cup of java to wake up was more urgent at the moment.

CHAPTER 7
(Friday, February 26, 2016)

George heard a voice calling his name from somewhere above him. He opened his eyes and glanced up at a nurse standing at the side of his bed. Gazing around the room, he noticed he was lying in a hospital bed. His left leg and chest were heavily bandaged. He wore an oxygen mask, and he had a needle in his right arm with IV fluids flowing into his battered body.

The nurse was talking to him. "Mr. Adams, how are you feeling?"

"I've had better days."

"Do you know where you are?"

"I'm in a hospital. By the way, what hospital is this?

"Penobscot County. You have some fairly serious injuries and the doctor had to do surgery to repair your femoral artery and spleen. You were lucky that your chest injury didn't require having your spleen removed. Are you in any pain right now?"

"No, but I have a headache. Can I get a Tylenol?"

"Let me see what the doctor has ordered." The nurse started to walk toward the door when George reached for her arm. "Please, can you tell me what's happened to my wife, Susan? Is she okay?"

"She's still in surgery. As soon as she is out, I'll make sure the doctor comes in to talk with you."

"Thank you."

George watched as the nurse left his room. He let his head fall back onto the pillow. His mind was instantly flooded with memories of the nightmare he and Susan had endured two nights ago. He worried about Susan and wondered if the baby was still alive. He tried to recall details about the attacker, but all he could remember was the guy was wearing a black mask, gloves, and a black trench coat. There was something familiar about him, yet George couldn't quite figure out what it was.

The nurse entered his room and interrupted his thoughts. Smiling, she handed him a small medication cup with two Tylenols and a glass of ice water.

He swallowed the tablets and thanked her.

"Mr. Adams, would you like something to eat?"

"Yes, please. A burger and fries would be great."

Still smiling, the nurse shook her head, "I believe you're on a clear liquid diet, so how about some jello and broth?"

George brought his hand up to his aching temples and waved the other hand toward the nurse. "Great. Whatever can cure you can also kill you, right?"

"Not very appetizing, yet hey, it's food, right?"

The nurse started to leave the room. Remembering

something, she turned back around and stood in the doorway. "By the way, there's a detective out in the hall who wants to talk to you. He was here two nights ago when the paramedics brought you here. Do you feel up to talking to him?"

"Sure, I can tell him what little I know, and find out that he knows even less."

Soon after the nurse left, a short, stocky, balding man strolled into his room and over to his bed. Extending his hand, he greeted George and they shook hands. "Hi, Mr. Adams. I'm Detective Mike Randolph with the Lakeland Police Department. I'm sorry about what happened to you and your wife." After his introduction, Randolph got right to the point.

"Over the past few days we have been investigating this case, and this is what we know so far:

1. You are being pursued by a serial killer, most likely someone who has a vendetta against those who served in the military in whatever fashion. We suspect this guy is either a former Marine, probably someone you know, or someone who has a gripe with you or your family.

2. There are other victims, as you already know. Dan Stevens, one of your squadron mates, was also attacked and his wife and daughter were killed. His one remaining daughter remains in critical condition in the hospital in Archer, Vermont.

3. These attacks and murders were committed by someone with a preference for using knives as his or her murder weapon."

"So, I have a few questions to ask you. I know you have been through a lot of trauma, including surgery, so I'll try to make this as short as possible. Do you have any questions for me at this point?"

George remained silent and thoughtful throughout the detective's report. His headache was subsiding, yet he felt dizzy and lightheaded from the effects of anesthesia. It was still difficult to talk, yet he felt compelled to be as helpful as possible to help bring the murderer to justice.

"Detective Randolph, you mentioned that the attacker most likely knows me. I served in Afghanistan from 2000-2004. Are you thinking that he was in my squadron? I was trying to recall as many details as possible and there was something familiar about this guy."

"Yes, that's the most likely possibility and a good place to start. Do you know anyone who could be holding any grudges against you?"

As he pondered the detective's question, he tried to recall scenes from fighting in Afghanistan, yet his brain still felt foggy from the anesthesia. Detective Randolph noticed the puzzled expression on George's face as he shook his head.

"I realize this is painful and difficult for you right now, but any details you can remember would be helpful. Perhaps, another question I have will help bring something to mind. As you tried to defend yourself, did you notice any identifying scars or other features? Can you describe the assailant?"

"Medium build and height. Wearing a full black mask covering his face and head, black gloves and trench coat. That's all I recall." Once again, George fell silent. He thought about Dan and wondered how he was surviving without his wife and daughter. He made a mental note to give him a call once he was feeling better and knew how Susan was doing.

The detective started jotting a few notes down on the notepad he pulled from his coat pocket. He then stood up and put on his coat. "Thanks, Mr. Adams, for all your help. That's all for today." He handed George his business card. "If you think of anything else, please call me. I'll be back tomorrow. Get some rest." He started walking toward the door.

Abruptly, George's mind was immersed with images of that horrific night. As he fought with the attacker, he caught glimpses of something metal flashing around the attacker's neck.

"Randolph, wait… George called out to the detective. I remember something else. He was wearing something around his neck. Possibly dog tags."

CHAPTER 8
(Friday February 26, 2016)

The storm was now in full swing, blanketing the roads in a damp, slick glaze of ice and thick, wet snow, making driving difficult. In the whiteout conditions, Samuels narrowed his eyes and strained to keep sight of the silver Ford Escort he was following. The car slipped a good distance ahead of him and disappeared from sight. He kept his foot on the accelerator, hoping to catch up with them, yet his Camaro kept swerving from one side of the road to the other. Luckily for him, there were no other cars on the road at 3:30 a.m. in the quaint neighborhood he drove through.

Without warning, his car started to spin out of control. He tried to turn the steering wheel in the opposite direction of the spin. The car kept swerving in a wild arc down the street until it finally came to a screeching halt on the sidewalk in front of someone's house. His hands were locked in a white-knuckled death grip on the steering wheel. His heart was pounding and he breathed heavily as he tried to steady himself.

After a few minutes, Samuels glanced around him and saw that the snowfall had slowed considerably. Breathing a sigh of relief, he placed his foot back on the accelerator, and slowly maneuvered the Camaro off the sidewalk back onto the street. He caught sight of the silver Ford Escort parked a few blocks ahead on the opposite side of the street. He breathed a sigh of relief. *Today's my lucky day,* he thought, *but not so much for them.* Staring out the pitted windshield, he scanned the area for any signs of neighborhood residents out for a late night walk, yet he saw no one.

Samuels got out of his Camaro and walked the two blocks to where the Escort was parked in the driveway of a white and tan two story house. He observed the house had upper and lower porches surrounded by white picket fences. Scanning the house, he approached the staircase leading up to the front door and ascended the stairs. The only sound he heard was the crunching of snow under his black sneakers as he reached the front door.

Pulling out his pen light and lock release gun from his trench coat pocket, he first tried the doorknob to see if it was open. Finding the door locked, he opened it with the lock release gun and stepped inside the house. Quietly closing and locking the door behind him, he stared into penetrating darkness surrounding him. He listened for sounds of movement upstairs and down, however heard only dead silence.

Pulling a larger flashlight from his pants pocket, he shined its bright beam ahead of him and scanned the house's layout. Noticing the frugally decorated front room ahead of him, he shined the beam to his right and noticed it led to two bedrooms and a guest bathroom. Samuels silently crept down the hallway and peered into the empty bathroom. He made his way to the nearest bedroom and slowly opened the door. Glancing around the room, he assumed it was a guest bedroom. He saw that the neatly made bed was empty. Continuing down the hall, he discovered the second bedroom door was wide open. Squinting his eyes, he scanned the room, only to find an empty bed once again.

Slowly making his way back to the front room, he beheld a large, muscular figure to his left, who leapt right out in front of him. The freight train blow to his jaw knocked him down to the floor. He landed with a loud thud that knocked the wind out of him, and sent his flashlight flying across the room.

Momentarily stunned, he glanced up at the large figure standing above him, and before another blow landed hard against his cheek, he grabbed the man's leg and pulled him down toward the floor. The man landed on top of him, his long hair sprawled across Samuels stunned face, blocking his view. Samuels flipped the guy over on his back, so that now Samuels was on top. He grabbed for his knife inside his vest pocket and covering the guy's mouth, stabbed him several times in the chest. Silas breathlessly waited for a few seconds, but the guy lie motionless on the floor beneath him.

Rolling his body off the guy, he stood up, keeping his eyes focused on the inert figure lying there. Suddenly his attention was diverted by the sound of soft, faint footsteps on the floor above him. He grinned. *You're next, sweetheart...*

Creeping softly upstairs, Samuels walked slowly down the hall toward the last bedroom straight ahead of him with its door closed. He slowly opened the door and peered in. The room was dark, except for the wide beam of light shining from Samuels flashlight. He scanned the room with his flashlight and caught a glimpse of the queen size bed. He also recognized the girl's facc who appeared to be fast asleep in the bed. Tip-toeing toward the bed, he heard one of the floorboards creek under his weight stopped dead in his tracks. Jennie's eyes were now wide open and she sat up in bed and stared at the figure standing only a few feet from the bed. "Is that you, Sean?" she hoarsely whispered. Samuels turned off the flashlight. "Guess again," he replied.

Jennie screamed and Samuels quickly ran toward the bed. Jennie, sensing his movement, rolled off the bed onto the floor. Shining his flashlight on the bed, he realized it was empty. He caught sight of Jennie running toward the door on the other side of the bed and flung himself toward her. He tackled her and landed on top of her. Reaching in his coat pocket, he pulled out a roll of duct tape and wrapped the tape around her mouth and head just in time to stifle her scream.

Jennie reached up with her right hand and swung it at his face with all her might. With her other hand she tried to pull off his mask, yet he grabbed her hands and pinned them down to the floor above her head. Momentarily stunned from the blow, he tasted blood dripping from his nose. "You're gonna regret that, Jennie," he warned.

Weariness now evident, Trace sat for a few minutes in her white Porsche parked in the convenience store lot and closed her eyes. After a few minutes, she opened them and stared at the dashboard clock. 4:06 a.m. She longed to be back in her house a few blocks from her office.

Mulling over the day's events, the guy pulling out of the parking lot suddenly came to mind. She recalled hearing something about a red Camaro on the news earlier at the High Five. *Wasn't that the same car they were looking for?* She remembered the driver's sinister stare as their eyes met, and she felt a strange uneasiness overcome her. *Could this dude be the perp,* she wondered?

Trace walked into the convenience store and greeted the short-haired, pimple-faced kid standing behind the counter. She slowly strolled over to the coffee counter and poured herself a cup of the strongest java she found. Passing on the cream, she reached for a lid, covered the steaming cup and sauntered back to the kid at the counter.

Handing him money for the coffee, she asked, "Do you remember a guy in a red Camaro coming into this store about a half hour ago?" Trace pulled out her badge from her purse and showed it to the kid.

"Yeah, I was starting my shift and he was leaving the store. I noticed him sitting in his Camaro and watching Jennie, the girl who worked the shift before me. Her boyfriend, Sean, picked her up and he followed them out of the lot. He was kind of creepy looking and walked with a limp."

Trace quickly glanced at his name tag. "Johnny, I need you to give me Jennie's address NOW! This guy is armed and dangerous!

"WOW! Okay, hold on a sec!" Johnny rushed into the break room to check the computer, and returned to the counter within minutes. He handed Trace a piece of paper. "Here's her address. She lives pretty close, just a few miles away on Grove St.

Hope you can find her before this guy does! Good luck, Detective!”

"Thanks! Trace shot back over her shoulder as she ran out the door. Racing to her car, she got in and drove toward the house on Grove St. Her GPS showed that the house was a few miles away.

Within 15 minutes, she reached Grove St. and turned right. She looked to her left searching for the address when something red caught her attention. She noticed it was a Camaro and shivered with anticipation, hoping it wasn't too late. Finding the address, she grabbed a flashlight from the back seat, locked her Porsche, and hurried up the driveway to the front door. Trace tried to open the door, but it was locked. She pulled a tension wrench from her coat pocket and poked at the lock a few times before the door finally opened. Breathing a sigh of relief, she shined her flashlight into the darkness of the house. Stopping dead in her tracks, she saw the silhouette of a large form lying on the floor a few feet ahead of her near the staircase on her left.

Slowly approaching the body, she observed it was a young guy with long black hair strewn across his face, lying motionless on his back in a pool of blood. *This must be Jennie's boyfriend, Sean,* she thought.

As she knelt over his inert body, she felt a faint pulse over his carotid artery. Shaking him, she called his name and detected that his eyes fluttered. Leaning over his mouth, she felt his ragged breath. Reaching in her coat pocket for her cell, she dialed 911. "Hello, 911. What's your emergency?" Hearing the operator's voice, she sprinted toward the bathroom, figuring her voice wouldn't be heard with the door shut. Quietly closing the door behind her, she kept her voice low as she spoke to the

operator. "There's an injured man who's bleeding and unconscious, and a woman who might also be hurt."

After giving the operator the address and her identifi-
cation, she ran out of the bathroom down the hall and into the
front room. Hearing a noise behind her, she stopped next to the
staircase and spun quickly around toward where she heard the
noise. Shining her flashlight into the surrounding darkness, she
heard some heavy footsteps on the floor above her followed by
a muffled scream.

Climbing the stairs two at a time, she reached the
second floor landing. She tip-toed her way down the hall past
one empty bedroom and a bathroom to the bedroom at the end
of the hallway. Taking her .45 semiautomatic pistol from her
shoulder holster, she slowly approached the last bedroom door.
Breathing heavily from fatigue and anticipating a fight, she
braced herself for her entrance. She felt sweat pouring down
her face as she took a wide stance with gun pointing toward the
door. The loud sound of something crashing against the door
stirred her to action. Running full bore toward the door, she
kicked the door open and burst into the bedroom.

Holding her flashlight in one hand, she scanned the
room and discovered Jennie sprawled half naked on the floor
with duct tape covering her mouth and Samuels lying on top of
her. He held her arms down with his massive hands. Her eyes
widened in panic as she saw Trace enter. Angrily looking up at
the intruder, he quickly rolled off Jennie and with his pants still
unzipped, charged at Trace like a raging bull.

Trace fired a bullet from her semiautomatic directly at
Silas' chest and saw him adeptly spin around to dodge the bullet. She kept shooting until he knocked her to the floor. Barely

breathing from the force of Samuels' attack, she rolled around with him as he tried to wrestle the gun from her hand. Samuels was now straddling her so she shined her flashlight in his face, momentarily blinding him. She kicked her legs up toward his face with every ounce of adrenaline in her body. Her leg thrust pushed him backward. He hit his head against the wall, and slumped over to the floor.

Trace looked over at him and noticed he was bleeding from his head and face wounds. Trace pushed herself up to a standing position with gun in tow and rushed over to where Jennie was lying. Signaling to the door, she grabbed Jennie's hand and pulled her off the floor. In a flash, they bolted toward the door and ran out into the hallway. Trace ran ahead of Jennie, and seeing lights in the front room, she peered down the staircase at the paramedics hovering over the wounded man. Breathing a sigh of relief, she yelled down to them. "Hey guys! Up here! This lady also needs help!"

Sprinting into the bathroom, she grabbed a towel and threw it to Jennie to cover herself. Remembering Silas, Trace ran down the hall. Glancing back over her shoulder, she saw a paramedic helping Jennie walk downstairs.

Holding her gun in front of her, she quickly entered the bedroom. Her gaze was focused on the floor where Silas was once lying, but instead she heard the sound of a shot fired at her. Instinctively dodging the bullet fired by Silas' gun, it missed her head by inches and blasted into the drywall behind her. She saw Silas running toward the window and shot toward his back. He ducked just in time as the bullet shattered the window. Opening the window, he artfully slid himself outside, rolled down the carport roof and jumped to the ground.

Trace ran over to the window in time to see him running down the street toward his Camaro. Silas got in his car and dodged the last bullet fired by Trace that shattered his windshield. "Until we meet again, asshole!" she yelled after him as he drove away.

Trace dragged her weary body downstairs and talked for a few minutes with the paramedics. She walked outside with them to the ambulance. Noticing that Jennie and her boyfriend were safe inside the ambulance, she turned and walked back to her car. She let out a sigh and drove down the street heading for home and the lure of a few hours of well-deserved shut eye. Reaching in her coat pocket for her cell, she dialed Sheriff Anderson's number. A groggy male voice answered. "Hello…

"Hey Sheriff, sorry to call so early, nevertheless we need to talk. I had an interesting encounter with someone you're gonna want to know about."

"Are you coming here?"

'No, I need to get a few hours of shut eye. It's been a busy night. You're making a special trip to my office. Say, around noon. Oh, yeah, and bring Dan with you."

CHAPTER 9
(Saturday, February 27, 2016)

Dan stood at Annie's bedside smoothing her long auburn hair with his hand. Her eyes were closed and her small freckled face was covered with an oxygen mask. Her chest was dotted with electrodes that were attached to a heart monitor. She wore a blood oxygen monitor device on the index finger of her right hand, and an IV was keeping her battered body nourished and hydrated.

Dr. Wilson stood next to Dan at Annie's bedside. Dan made daily trips to the hospital to be with Annie and it was wearing on him. Dr. Wilson gave him daily reports on her progress and spoke with Dan when he arrived at 9 a.m. Before entering Annie's room in ICU, Dr. Wilson informed him that they had removed Annie's breathing and chest tubes earlier that morning. Dan longed for Annie to be well enough for him to care for her at home.

"How much longer do you think she needs to stay in the hospital?" Dan asked.

"She's still got a long road ahead of her, yet she's now able to breathe on her own. This is a significant improvement and very encouraging," Dr. Wilson replied.

"Can she hear me when I talk to her?"

"Yes, she's still heavily sedated, but she can hear you."

Dan leaned over and kissed Annie on her cheek. "Annie, please hang in there for your daddy. I love you so much, sweetheart. You're all I've got right now." Dan was instantly overcome with emotion and tears streamed down his face as he looked up at Dr. Wilson.

"You know, when she was born, she was breech and almost didn't make it. Peggy was in labor for over thirty hours and was having a difficult time trying to deliver. The doctor attempted to reposition her, yet that was unsuccessful. Peggy had to have a C-Section. They both had to stay a few days longer in the hospital. With Stephanie, it was a lot easier." Dr. Wilson patted Dan on the shoulder. "She's a fighter just like her dad." He smiled at Dan.

"When do you think she'll be able to open her eyes?"

"Hard to say. Most likely, once the sedative medication wears off, she could open her eyes at any time. I think I'll give you two some alone time."

"Thanks for everything, Dr. Wilson." They shook hands. He watched as the doctor left the room and pulled out a handkerchief to wipe his tear-stained face. Sitting down on the chair next to Annie's bed, he reached for her hand and gave it a gentle squeeze.

Looking around the room, he heard the steady beeping of the heart monitor and looked up at the monitor trying to decipher its puzzling wave patterns. There was something reassuring about the steady rhythm. The room was barely large enough to hold Annie's bed and over bed table, and smelled of some antiseptic cleaning fluid. Directing his gaze at Annie, he saw her eyes were still closed. Studying her face, he thought he saw her eyelids flickering. She suddenly coughed and moaned into the breathing mask covering her face.

Dan sprang to his feet. "Annie, it's daddy. Can you open your eyes?"

Annie's eyelids flickered again and then slowly opened her brown eyes. Gazing at Dan, she had a puzzled expression on her face as though she didn't recognize him.

Dan quickly approached Annie's bed and gently scooped Annie into his outstretched arms. "Daddy, where am I?" Annie gasped and tightly wrapped her arms around his neck. Dan lovingly embraced her and gently stroked her hair with his hand.

"You're in the hospital baby, but you're gonna be okay!"

The realization of the moment hit them at the same time and tears were streaming down their faces. Annie pulled herself away from Dan and solemnly stared at him while bravely holding back tears.

"Daddy, why am I here?"

"Sweetheart, you were hurt pretty bad, but you're doing better. Try to rest as much as possible and that will help you get well faster."

Dan bent over to kiss her cheek and she hugged his neck. Gazing into his eyes, she wiped her face and stopped crying. "Will you stay with me, Daddy?"

"Yes, sweetheart. I promise. Get some rest now, okay?"

Nodding her head, she closed her eyes and was soon fast asleep.

Dan's cell phone rang and he hurried outside Annie's room to assure the phone call didn't wake her. Peeking inside at her still asleep, he answered the call.

It was Sheriff Anderson. "Hello Dan. Hey, are you busy right now?"

"I'm at the hospital with Annie. What's up?"

"I didn't mean to interrupt, but I need you to come in to my office as soon as you can. I heard from Trace and it sounds like she has some important information to tell us about your case. She wants to meet us at her office by noon if possible."

Checking his watch, he noticed it was almost 10 a.m. "I'll be there as soon as I can." Casting a quick glance at Annie's motionless form, he rushed down the hall toward the elevator and rode it down to the lobby. Sprinting outside to his Mustang, he raced over to the sheriff's office a few miles away from the hospital located in downtown Archer.

CHAPTER 10
(Saturday, February 27, 2016)

When Dan arrived, Sheriff Anderson was waiting in his white SUV and he signaled to Dan to get in. They headed north on Highway 7 toward Waterton.

The sheriff greeted Dan and asked, "How's Annie doing?"

"She's doing better. They removed her breathing and chest tube this morning, and she's now awake. Dr. Wilson said she still has a long recovery, but at least she's making improvement." Dan let out a long sigh of relief.

The sheriff's mouth curled into a smile. "Glad to hear that, Dan. She's been in a coma for the past week, right?"

"Yeah… we didn't think she was ever gonna come out of it, but I had to have faith. She's all I've got now…" his voice cracked with emotion and trailed off.

Dan and the sheriff were silent for a few minutes, both

lost in their own thoughts. Dan thought of Peggy and Stephanie and his eyes once again welled with tears. He missed them more than words could express. Remembering the funeral preparations Gina was making for the next day, he told the sheriff about it, and he nodded to Dan.

Suddenly, George and Susan came to mind and he wondered about their situation. As if reading Dan's mind, the sheriff replied, "Dan, I have some news about George and I thought this might be a good time to tell you. I heard from a detective up in Maine who's working on the Adams case. Name is Mike Randolph. He called me late yesterday and said he spoke with George, who's still in the hospital."

Turning to look at the sheriff, Dan interrupted him. "How is he? How's Susan?"

"Apparently, their injuries were pretty serious and they both had surgery. I don't know about Susan or her baby. George was able to talk to the detective and told him that he remembered the attacker was wearing dog tags around his neck. Ring any bells?"

Dan stared at the sheriff with a surprised expression. He thought there was something familiar about the attacker, yet he couldn't quite figure out what it was. This just confirmed it had to be someone in his squadron. His mind feverishly pictured the faces of his comrades and immediately the face of Samuels appeared with amazing clarity.

He flashed back to Afghanistan and was instantly transported back there. He recalled when he, Griffin, and Master Sergeant Nielson ran through a barrage of gunfire and explosions through the town streets. Running past ruined buildings, the choking smell of smoke, and visions of bloodied bodies of

Taliban soldiers sprawled on the ground flashed through his mind. He remembered running into the burned out shelter and encountering George kneeling over a wounded Samuels. He vividly remembered George reporting that Samuels tried to desert the squadron, and his court-martial. Everything made sense.

"Yeah, they're ringing loud and clear. One guy on my squad, Silas Samuels, comes to mind. He freaked out on us when the going got tough and tried to run. George ran after him and saved this miserable scumbag's life. We testified against him in court as a deserter. He served some time in prison and so he's now getting his revenge."

The sheriff looked thoughtful and pondered Dan's statement for a few minutes.

"It sure sounds like the guy has a motive, but are you sure this guy is the murderer? Could you pick him out for certain among other suspects?"

"Trust me, Sheriff. When you spend two years with someone, sleep in the same barracks, do the same drills, eat the same slop, defend and rely on that person, you get to know how he ticks."

"Dan, I'm sure you got to know your squad mates well, especially in combat. You served with him fifteen years ago and haven't seen him since, right? I'm just trying to play devil's advocate here."

Dan nodded and fell silent for a few moments and looked out the window as they drove past the snow-packed Vermont countryside. As they drove, he wondered if he would remember Silas. People change with the passing of time. *Silas sure as hell remembers us,* he realized.

Still gazing out the window, he noticed the wintery landscape had now changed to the icy, grey waterline of Lake Champlain that bordered the town of Waterton. He recalled walking with Peggy a few years ago in Waterfront Park along the beautiful lavender flower lined sidewalk that led through the park.

The sheriff interrupted his thoughts. "Okay, we're here." He parked in the lot in front of a small, quaint redbrick one story building. Dan looked at the buildings in the neighborhood admiring their picturesque New England architecture. As they approached her office, he looked forward to seeing Trace again and wondered what information she had to share.

Sheriff Anderson opened the white door leading to Trace's office and Dan followed him in. A bell signaled their entrance. Dan glanced around at the bright white walls adorned with lifelike seascape paintings and a brown plastic sign on the wall above her desk that read: Detective At Work: Enter At Your Own Risk. Dan chuckled and continued scanning the office. He noticed Trace's desk had a stack of papers lying in a neat pile to one side and a bunch of family pictures on the other side. In the middle of her desk sat her name plate that read: DETECTIVE TRACE MALONE. The smell of fragrant perfume filled the air.

Trace entered from a small foyer behind several strands of beads hanging from the ceiling. She smiled and wearily nodded at them. She was wearing a sharp looking plum blazer with matching pants, and a light pink blouse underneath the blazer. Her medium length blonde hair was tied in a ponytail with a few blonde strands hanging down in wisps over her eyes. Both men stared at her a bit longer than either had intended. She sat down at her desk and brushed a few strands of hair behind her ears.

"You'll have to excuse me. It was a long night last night and I didn't get much sleep," she apologized. She motioned toward wooden straight back chairs in front of her desk. "Please sit down, guys. This will take a while. Can I get you anything to drink?"

Sheriff Anderson walked toward the back room. "I can help myself, Trace, no need to get up. Dan, how about you?"

"Water is good with some ice. Thanks, Sheriff."

Trace and Dan's eyes met.

Dan broke the silence. "Good seeing you again, Detective. Trace smiled and kept her gaze on him. "You as well, Dan. How is Annie doing?"

"She's slowly improving. Dr. Wilson removed her breathing and chest tubes this morning. She's now able to talk a bit. I was wondering if she would even recognize me when she finally opened her eyes."

"Good to hear." Trace breathed a sigh of relief. "She's been through hell and back. This is great news! I'm happy that she's back on the road to recovery and I'll bet you are as well."

"Yeah. I'm trying to take it one day at a time. Dr. Wilson said she still has a long road ahead of her, but at least we can now see the light at the end of the tunnel."

"And it's not an oncoming freight train," Trace teased. They both shared a laugh.

Sheriff Anderson entered the room holding their drinks and gave Dan his glass of water. Glancing at Trace as he sat in his chair, he got right to the point. "So, what have you got for us?"

Trace leaned back in her brown swivel chair and let out a long sigh. "Okay, so I was driving back from Archer last night and I needed some coffee. As I pulled into the convenience store parking lot, I saw a guy in a red Camaro pulling out. We briefly glanced at each other, and at first it didn't register. I sat in my car thinking about the day's events, and suddenly remembered the news I heard earlier at High Five mentioned a red Camaro. So, I grabbed a quick cup of coffee and got the name and address of the store clerk who this guy followed home. Her name is Jennie Andrews and her boyfriend is Sean Johnson."

Dan and the sheriff leaned back in their chairs listening to Trace's story. The sheriff pulled a notepad from his shirt pocket and jotted down a few notes.

"So, I rushed over to the house on Grove St. and on the way saw this guy's red Camaro parked a few blocks away. I got there just in time to find Sean lying on the floor of the front room near the staircase leading up to the second floor. He was unconscious and had several stab wounds to his chest. Sean gave a good fight, I'm sure. I called 911 and they came while I was upstairs dealing with our perp. She paused to catch her breath as she recalled the wrestling match she had with the man.

Dan leaned toward her with interest. "Did you notice anything around his neck?"

Returning his gaze, she shook her head. "No. It was pretty dark in the upstairs bedroom and he wore a black trench coat, mask and gloves. He was straddling Jennie and was obviously trying to rape her, until I changed the scenario."

Sheriff Anderson shifted impatiently in his chair. "What

happened to the perp?"

"When I kicked him off me, he hit his head pretty hard against the wall and was unconscious for a while. I grabbed Jennie and got us both the hell outta there and gave her to the paramedics who arrived while I was dealing with mask boy. I ran back to the bedroom and fired a shot at him that missed and hit the window. He escaped out the window, rolled off the carport roof, and jumped down into the street. I fired another shot and hit his windshield. Son of a bitch!" Trace's face blushed bright red with anger.

Dan and the sheriff stared intently at her pondering her story for a few moments. Dan understood that she wanted to catch the guy as much as he did. He smiled at her. "At least you were able to save a couple of lives." He noticed her deep green eyes focusing on him and the angry expression changed to an embarrassed pout. "Well, yeah, you're right, but the perp got away."

Sheriff Anderson interjected. "Well, don't be too hard on yourself. We know who this guy is Trace. Dan remembered one of his squadron mates, Silas Samuels, tried to desert the team in the midst of combat in Afghanistan back in 2001. They testified against him during his trial. He was court-martialed and served time in prison. So, there's the motive. We also know that another of his comrades, George, and his wife, Susan, were attacked and are now in the hospital up in Maine. The detective working on their case called me and shared some information that George told him."

Dan leaned forward toward Trace. "That's why I asked if you noticed something around his neck. When the sheriff told me it was dog tags, Silas immediately came to my mind."

Trace was now writing down some notes on her note-pad as Dan was talking. Looking up from her notes, she pondered what the sheriff and Dan told her and smiled.

"Great work, guys! So now we need to find Silas and keep him from doing more damage, right? I had a feeling this guy was someone in the Marines."

"You were right, as usual." The sheriff smiled and glanced at Trace. He then turned his head back toward Dan. "I think your other squadron mates are in danger, Dan. Do you know their whereabouts?"

"I've kept in contact with Master Sergeant Nielson and Griffin. Nielson used to live in the upper peninsula of Michigan, and when we last talked about a year ago, he said he bought a house in Northern Vermont after leaving the Marines in 2004. He invited me to come for a visit. Griffin visited a few years ago when he was skiing in the Green Mountains. He now lives in the Adirondacks area."

"You need to contact them and let them know about Silas. He could pay them a visit at any time, or, he could take some time to cool off and plan his next attack."

Dan nodded at the sheriff. "I will try to connect when we get back to Archer."

Trace listened as Dan and Sheriff Anderson bantered back and forth. Unconsciously twirling her pen, she recalled all that happened the previous night. She felt tired and sore all over from her encounter with Silas and not getting much sleep. She felt sorry for his victims, yet also wondered if there was more to his story than what Dan had shared about their time in the Marines. She made a mental note to check the autopsy and lab reports on the knife Silas left behind at Dan's house. The sheriff's voice brought her back to the present.

"Trace, do you have anything else to add before we end our meeting?"

She noticed Dan and the sheriff were both staring at her. There was something tender and appealing in Dan's eyes, and she returned his gaze.

"Sorry, guys. My mind was elsewhere for a moment. I do have one thing. Dan, if you can please call me in a few days. I still need to review the lab and autopsy reports and go over them with you." She handed him a business card and taking the card, his hand brushed against her fingers.

"Yes, certainly." He nodded and their eyes met once again.

Standing up from their chairs, Dan and the sheriff thanked and shook hands with Trace and left her office.

After they left, Trace sat back down at her desk and once again her thoughts focused on Dan. She felt an instant attraction to him, yet realizing their present situation quickly dismissed those thoughts.

CHAPTER 11
(Monday, February 29, 2016)

Silas walked into Jose's Car Painting Shop in Waterton. He walked up to the counter and talked to the owner of the shop. Jose was of Spanish descent, around thirty years of age, with a solid muscular build and long, shoulder length black hair. He greeted Silas and extended his hand. After they shook hands, Silas asked how long it would take to have his car painted silver.

"We're pretty busy right now, so the earliest I could have it ready is tomorrow morning. Is that okay?"

"I'm kind of in a hurry. I need to get out of town as soon as possible, you know?"

"Let me talk with my partner."

"I have nowhere to stay." Silas stood his ground.

"You do now." Jose handed him a business card of the nearest La Plata Inn a few blocks down the street from his shop. "Ask for Tony and he'll take good care of you. Just mention my name. I send him many of my customers. He's the manager there."

"So, what time tomorrow will it be ready?"

"Depends on what you want done. We can even change driver's license, and the VIN number and plates of the vehicle if you want."

Silas thought for a moment. "How much do you charge?"

"Normally, we charge $1500.00 for our complete package, but for you, it's $1200.00 with cash down."

"Okay, here you go." Silas pulled out a wad of cash from his coat pocket and paid Jose. "So, what time tomorrow can I pick up the car?"

"You can talk to Tony and work out the arrangements."

Silas nodded his head. "See you tomorrow." They shook hands and after turning over the car key to Jose, Silas left the shop and headed down the street toward La Plata Inn.

Arriving at the Inn, Silas approached the stocky, middle aged woman at the reception desk and checked in. He then asked if Tony was available. The woman picked up the phone and tried his extension, and told him Tony was at dinner. "Are you a friend of Tony's?" the woman asked.

"Well, a friend of a friend you might say." The woman gave him a puzzled look.

"I am having some work done on my car in the neighborhood, and I asked the owner where I could stay for the night while my car is worked on. He directed me to Tony," Silas explained.

"Oh, okay. I'll let Tony know you're looking for him,

Mr. Samuels. Your room is on the main floor, room 110." She pointed toward the hall on her left and handed him the key.

"Thanks." Suddenly feeling hungry, he decided to grab something to eat before going to his room. "I think I'll grab a burger first," he replied to the woman. She smiled at Silas and replied, "There's a great burger place down the street called Hank's Hamburgers."

Smiling, he thanked her and hurried out the door. Walking down the busy street, he checked out the neighborhood and noticed the area was pretty run down. He saw several red brick apartment buildings that housed senior citizens and low income residents, and passed a few thrift stores and empty storefronts that were out of business.

He noticed an elderly man standing in front of a thrift store holding a sign in one hand and the leash of an emaciated looking brown, short-haired dog in the other. Squinting his eyes, Silas nodded toward the man and noticed his sign said, "Vietnam Vet. Anything will help." Silas reached into his coat pocket and finding some change, tossed it into the man's open backpack lying on the ground as he passed by. "God bless you." The man focused his piercing blues eyes on Silas, as his withered and sunburned face cracked a smile.

Reaching Hank's, he walked in and was greeted by a curvaceous waitress in her early twenties with curly black hair and glasses. She smiled and greeted him. "Party of one?" He nodded and followed her down the aisle toward a small table at the back of the restaurant. She handed him a menu and he sat down at the table. Still smiling and chewing gum the waitress asked, "Need a few minutes?"

Nodding his head, Silas looked briefly at the menu.

As the waitress hurried away from his table, he stared intently at her short, tight uniform and long legs. *She's a pretty young thing,* he thought. After studying the menu for a few minutes, he noticed the waitress approaching his table.

"What will it be tonight?" she asked smiling and chewing her gum. Silas ordered a double cheeseburger and fries. Glancing at her buxom figure, he asked, "Are you working late tonight?"

"Yeah, really late. Is that all, sir?"

"Well, let's see…" Silas suddenly caught sight of two uniformed policemen who entered the restaurant. "Be back in a few," she interrupted him and rushed toward the officers. They scanned the restaurant so Silas hid his face behind the menu. *Damn,* he cursed to himself. *Wonder why they're in here?* He took a quick glance from behind the menu and noticed the waitress led the cops to a table across the restaurant from where he sat.

Silas casually got up from his seat and walked toward the front of the restaurant. He observed in his peripheral vision that the waitress was talking with the officers. After taking their orders, she glanced over at Silas standing near the door and approached him. "Sorry sir, it's kind of busy tonight," she apologized. "Didn't mean to ignore you."

"No worries. I saw you were busy with the officers."

"Yeah, they're regulars. Are you leaving?"

"Yes, I just got a call from my boss and I need to get back to the office. I'll just take my order to go."

Silas nervously shifted his weight. Sensing his uneasiness, she studied his face for a brief moment. "Okay. I understand working late. Be back with your order in a few." She hurried toward the grill near the door and placed his order. Silas casually turned his head in the direction of where the officers were seated and noticed they were involved in their conversation. The waitress returned within five minutes and handed him the order. He paid the waitress, who was also the cashier, and hurried outside.

The cold wind bit into his face and he felt light snowflakes hitting his eyelashes as he hurried down the street. Pulling up the collar of his trench coat, he finally reached the motel. Entering, he nodded at the woman behind the desk and she called out to him. "Mr. Samuels, Tony just headed down to your room." Hunger pangs were now gnawing at his stomach. He muttered under his breath and nodded toward the woman. "Thanks."

As Silas approached his room, he saw a tall, thin, slightly balding man in the hall knocking at his door. The man turned to face him and their eyes locked. He spoke first. "Mr. Samuels?"

"Yes. Are you Tony?"

The man nodded and extended his hand. They shook hands and stood for a few moments in the hall surveying each other. Tony broke the silence. "Jose told me you are having your car worked on and wanted some further information from me. Welcome to our humble abode." He smiled and glanced at the Hank's Hamburger bag Silas held in his gloved hand. "Sorry for interrupting your dinner."

"No worries, Tony." He wanted to talk with Tony about the whole car package. "Would you like to come in for a few minutes? We can talk while I eat if you don't mind."

"Sure, no problem."

Silas pulled out the room key and opened the door. Tony walked in first and Silas followed. Silas glanced around at his customary no frills motel room and walked over to a small table next to the TV in the middle of the room. He sat down in the black swivel chair next to the table. He quickly reached into his food bag and pulled out a double cheeseburger wrapped in foil. He ripped off the wrapper and hungrily bit into the juicy sandwich.

Tony sat down behind him on the bed. "So, where are you from?" he asked Silas. Turning around to face Tony, he replied, "Originally from Pennsylvania. What about you?"

"Lived here in Waterton all my life."

Silas nodded and munched on another big chunk of burger. He devoured the rest of his burger and woofed down a handful of fries.

Silas stared at Tony for a few moments. "So, Tony, Jose told me you and he are business partners. What services do you provide and how long will it take?"

"Are you in a hurry?"

"Yeah. I need to see a friend in the Adirondacks, and Jose told me I could have this done by tomorrow."

Tony shook his head. "So, for new plates, VIN, new ID, and dismantling the GPS, this will take a good part of tomorrow. I could have it ready by early Wednesday morning."

Silas held his ground. "Any chance I can get the car by tomorrow afternoon? This is urgent." Reaching into his holster, he brought out his M9 Beretta semi-automatic pistol and pointed it at Tony's head.

Tony stared back at Silas and held his hands in the air. "Whoa! Hey, tomorrow afternoon is no problem. I'd better get started." Glancing at his watch, he noticed it was almost 10 p.m. He slowly got up off the bed and stared at Silas' gun. A slight smile crossed his face as Silas placed the gun on the table. "Good thing that's a Beretta and not a standard issue. So, at least you're not a cop."

"Today's your lucky day, Tony." Silas gathered all his food wrappings from the table, wadded them in a ball and tossed them in the garbage can underneath the table. He then frowned when he remembered his experience at Hank's earlier that evening. "I'm not a cop, but I saw two of them at Hank's and they interrupted a potential date with this hot waitress."

Tony was silent for a moment as he pondered Silas' comment and studied his face. The sinister stare and wry smile were unnerving. Tony walked backward toward the door, keeping his focus on Silas. Opening the door, he nervously smiled. "Have a good night and I'll see you tomorrow around 4 p.m." Silas nodded. Tony left the room and closed the door. He hurried down the hall, nodded to the woman at the front desk, and left the motel. As he raced out the door, he heard the woman call out to him. "Another late night, Tony?" Running down the dark street toward Jose's Garage, he thought, *if she only knew…*

After Tony left his room, Silas grabbed the TV remote and started flipping channels. He watched about an hour of an old Alfred Hitchcock movie, but found it was hard to keep his eyes open. He fell into a deep sleep for a few hours, and suddenly was awakened by a male voice in his room. It was a reporter on the twelve midnight news.

"…the East Coast killer strikes again. A 21 year old

woman, Jennie Andrews, and her boyfriend, 24 year old Sean Johnson, were found by paramedics three days ago and were taken to Waterton Memorial Hospital in serious condition." Half asleep, Silas listened to the reporter with a casual disinterest. He tried to focus his weary eyes on the bright TV screen as pictures of his latest victims were shown. "This killer was last seen in Lakeland, Maine driving a 2010 red Camaro and the Lakeland Police were able to trace the license plates. EX-MAR 5521. This man is now thought to still be in the Waterton area…"

Silas was now fully awake as a pencil sketch drawing of a man who bore a striking resemblance to himself flashed across the screen. "The Waterton Police are asking anyone who might have seen this man or his car to contact them at the following number…" Silas sprang up from the bed and turned off the TV.

Pacing around the room, his mind flooded with scattered thoughts . . . . *What if the cops he saw earlier at Hank's were onto him? Who identified him? Was it the waitress or was it Jennie? I need to make fast tracks out of here!*

Rushing over to his trench coat draped over the arm of the swivel chair, he pulled out his cell and pack of cigarettes and dialed Jose's number. Nervously glancing back over his shoulder at his briefcase lying on the bed, he listened while Jose's voice was heard on the answering machine. *Damn, where are they?*

Making his way back to the bed, he sat down and lit a cigarette. *This would calm him down. Smoking always did.* He pulled his briefcase closer to him, opened it, and blankly stared at the bloodied knife and picture of his next target, Sergeant

Griffin. He picked up the wallet size photo of a smiling Griffin and blew smoke at his face. "You're next, Sergeant."

Closing the briefcase, he put it on the floor next to his bed and reminded himself to clean the knife first thing in the morning. Stabbing his cigarette butt into the ashtray on the nightstand, he watched the last wisps of smoke dissipate into the air. His eyes heavy with the sleep he longed for, he laid down on the bed and soon fell into a deep slumber.

Sometime toward morning, he awoke from a dream hearing someone yell. Lying in bed in a cold sweat and shivering with fear, he realized the yell he heard was his own. Reliving the dream, he once again saw the familiar flashbacks of himself as a small boy. This time he was lying in a dark closet with duct tape covering his mouth so he couldn't scream. Pieces of wire were binding his hands together behind his back. His eyes welled up with tears as he felt the searing pain on his raw skin as he struggled to free his hands. *Who was the man who was beating him and touching his genitals night after endless night?*

Another horrid vision flashed before his weary eyes of his mother and father fighting. He saw his father drink another swig of vodka before he punched her again in the face. She grabbed for the bottle of vodka and smashed it against his face, leaving a deep, bloody gash on his cheek. Now filled with rage, he raced toward her and pushed her backward with full force. She stumbled and fell, hitting her head hard on the stone fireplace wall behind her. With horror, he recalled witnessing his mother lying on the floor with blood pouring out of a gaping fatal wound on her head. Peering in terror at the horrific scene from around the corner in the next room, he observed the expression of amusement on his father's face. He recognized it belonged to the same man who was assaulting him.

Silas recalled during his childhood, his mother and father brought him with them to weekly therapy sessions, yet his fear of his father kept him from revealing the dark family secrets. The realization of his father being his abuser made him angry. His dad's constant drinking only added more fuel to the fire, and he could now understand how his dad's behavior influenced his own.

Silas glanced at the clock on the nightstand shining its red iridescent glow into the darkened room. 5:45 a.m. He got out of bed and groggily stumbled into the bathroom. Turning on the light, he stared at himself in the mirror and noticed his facial hair was steadily forming the beginnings of a goatee and moustache. He realized it was at least a week or more since he last shaved. He let out a loud chuckle, as he fingered the thick stubble growing on his chin and upper lip. *The cops will never find me now!*

Silas showered and afterward he felt more awake and full of energy. He washed off his knife in the sink and took extra time to make sure it was nice and sharp for his next victim.

CHAPTER 12
(Tuesday, March 1, 2016)

At exactly 9 a.m., Trace raced into the white tile-floored main lobby of Waterton Memorial Hospital and hurried toward the information desk. She flashed her badge at the elderly gentleman sitting behind the desk and asked for Sean Johnson's room number.

He informed Trace that Sean was in the ICU and pointed toward the elevator across the hallway from where his desk was situated in the middle of the lobby. Thanking him, she glanced around at the brightly lit lobby with its windows strewn with flowered plants of every variety. She made her way toward the elevator and expecting a wait, she was surprised when the door quickly opened. Entering the elevator, she pressed the button and rode up to the fifth floor.

After walking down the long hallway toward the ICU, she entered the unit and heard the synchronous beeping of heart monitors mixed with whooshing sounds of respirators. She then noticed several nurses scurrying around behind the desk situated in the middle of the unit.

As she approached the desk, she thought to herself, *I could never do this kind of demanding work.* She almost laughed aloud when she realized that her work was also pretty demanding.

Stepping up to the desk, she again flashed her badge at the nurses and asked about the condition of Sean Johnson. One heavy set nurse with glasses and bright red hair, stood up from her computer and remarked, "He's still on the respirator and heavily sedated, so unable to respond to any questions." Noticing Trace's disappointment, she added, "You can still see him for a few minutes if you need to. His girlfriend, Jennie, is visiting." She pointed to the private room behind the nurse's station and hurried back to her seat at the computer.

Thanking the nurse, Trace entered the room and observed Sean lying motionless in bed with a breathing tube down his throat. Approaching him, she greeted Jennie who was sitting on the bed next to him with her back facing Trace. She was wearing a cast on her right hand. Jennie glanced over her shoulder at Trace. She could see Jennie's left eye was swollen shut and tears were streaming down her battered face. Recognizing Trace, she tried to smile and extended her left hand toward Trace. "Oh, my God, Detective Malone! Thanks so much for coming here. I'm so grateful… you saved my life and Sean's!"

"First of all, Jennie, you're welcome. I'm sorry that I didn't get there sooner for you both. Have you had a chance to speak to the doctor yet?"

Jennie solemnly nodded. "Yes, he was just in here about a half hour ago. He told me that Sean's injuries are pretty serious, with blood surrounding his heart and lungs…" She paused mid-sentence and tried to regain her composure. "He said Sean's not in any pain, and that once he starts breathing on his own, the breathing tube will be removed and he'll be able to talk."

Trace tried to console her by gently patting her arm.

"I know this is very traumatic for you, Jennie, yet do you think you can answer a few questions?" Jennie nodded. She waved her hand toward two chairs in one corner of the room and they both walked over and sat down.

As Trace started to speak, Jennie interrupted. "Have they caught the asshole yet?" Her face flushed with anger.

"Sadly, no, but I gave a description to the police of the guy I saw driving after you when I pulled into the convenience store parking lot that night. I also gave a description of the car he drove and they were able to trace his plates. I've been watching the news and last night I saw a pencil sketch drawing of the guy. So, we have a suspect, yet I'm not at liberty to divulge his name yet. We'll catch him, Jennie. It's just a matter of time."

Jennie let out a long sigh and gazed intently at Trace. "I hope so, Detective.

"Did you notice anything else about this guy? Even the smallest detail would be helpful."

Jennie thought back to that horrific night as tears once again welled up in her eyes.

"When he was on top of me, I tried to pull off his mask and briefly caught a glimpse of some hair on his chin, yet he grabbed my hand before I could pull it completely off his face. That's when he slammed my hand to the floor and broke my wrist. He also punched me in the face." She was now sobbing. Trace once again patted her arm. "Jennie, I'm sorry this happened to you, but I need to ask if anything else comes to mind about him?"

Still sobbing, she gingerly wiped her discolored face with her t-shirt and tried to recall more details about her attacker.

"I… I think he was wearing something metal around his neck. I could hear it jingling…" her voice trailed off into another sob.

Trace busily wrote some notes down on her notepad.

"Before coming here today, I talked with Officer Patterson, the officer who interviewed you that night, and he didn't mention this to me." Any reason you didn't mention this to him?"

"I was scared, and to be honest, that was the last thing I had on my mind." Pulling out a tissue from her purse, she blew her nose with her good hand. She dried her tears and seemed a bit calmer.

Trace pushed a wisp of her blonde hair behind her ear, as was her habit. "I understand." Looking down at the brown envelope in her lap, she quickly remembered the report the officer gave her at their meeting. She lowered her voice to almost a whisper.

"I just want you to know that the initial rape report came back with evidence of DNA findings. That means that this evidence can be further tested to see if it matches the DNA of the suspect." Jennie stared at Trace with a puzzled expression on her face.

"Is that a good thing?"

Trace smiled at Jennie. "Yes, Jennie. Forensic testing makes it more likely that the suspect will be identified and brought to justice. I recommend you follow up with your doctor who will do a blood test to make sure you're not pregnant. He will also do further testing to make sure you don't have a sexually transmitted disease."

Remembering she was supposed to meet Dan later that morning, she glanced at her watch and noticed it was almost 10:30 a.m.

Leaning over toward Jennie, Trace handed her a business card. "I need to leave for another meeting. If you think of anything else, please give me a call and keep me posted on Sean's progress."

"Thanks so much, Detective Malone, for all you have done!" Jennie stood up and flung her arms around Trace. After they embraced for a few moments, Trace looked directly at Jennie. "We'll get him, I promise!" She hurried out of Sean's room and left the hospital, heading toward her car.

As she sped out of the parking lot, her heart also raced in anticipation of meeting with Dan.

Gina, Wes, and Harley, their high energy border collie, stood outside the cabin where Dan stayed admiring the exquisite craftsmanship of the structure. Gina, like Dan, missed her dad, yet felt his strong presence while gazing at the cabin he built years ago. Gina walked up to the white pine entranceway and knocked on the door. She had talked with Dan earlier that morning and he invited her and Wes over. She was excited as always to spend time and catch up with her brother.

After a few minutes, Dan opened the door and greeted them with a smile. It had been a busy morning. He got up at 6 a.m. for a short stroll through the forest as was his usual routine since that fateful night. Strolling through the forest and being in nature calmed him and provided a welcome distraction from feeling the deep heartache of loss. After a shower and break-fast, he called George, who was still in the hospital, and told him that he and Trace would be visiting him later that after-noon. Trace asked to accompany Dan as she wanted to meet George and had questions to ask him.

Dan also left messages for Sergeant Griffin and Master Sergeant Nielson to alert them about Silas.

"Hey, sis, Wes! He gathered them into a group bear hug and they followed him into the cabin. Harley let out an excited bark and jumped at Dan, practically knocking him off his feet. "Hey, Harley girl!" he petted Harley's furry head and watched as she practically flew past Dan into the cabin.

Dan was the first to speak. "Gina, thanks so much for taking over the funeral arrangements. I thought you did a great job and appreciate that you had the reception at your house. I thought the church service went well and it was good seeing mom again. It was also good seeing friends and neighbors at the reception. I just wish it wasn't under these circumstances." Dan's eyes stung with tears he tried to hold back as he recalled the funeral service and the reception that followed. The pastor at their church gave a beautiful eulogy. Gina embraced her brother and afterwards wiped a few tears from her eyes. They stood face to face.

"Isn't that what family is for? I'm glad to help out in

whatever way I can. It was great seeing mom again. We don't get much time to spend with her with our busy work schedules. She looks good and I'm happy to see she's taking care of herself and keeping busy with her volunteer work at the community food bank. She actually helped me with the funeral arrangements."

Dan thanked her again and signaled to them to sit on the couch as he settled into a comfy brown corduroy rocker chair next to the fireplace. Harley flung herself down on the floor and curled into a big hairy ball at Dan's feet. She gazed up at Dan with her full attention and tongue hanging out. Dan bent forward to pet Harley's soft black and white furry head.

"Sorry, Gina, life's been pretty crazy as of late. I've had several meetings with Sheriff Anderson and a detective he called in to work on the case. I've also been spending a lot of time walking in the woods behind the cabin and trying to sort things out."

Wes spoke next. "How's Annie doing?" He leaned forward with a look of concern on his face.

"She's slowly improving. She's breathing on her own and the doctor removed the chest tube. She's also able to talk now." Dan paused as he realized how close he came to almost losing her as well. "According to Dr. Wilson, she still has a long road to hoe, yet she's pretty strong."

"I guess it runs in the family!" Gina exclaimed, her face beaming.

"This is good to hear, Dan," Wes replied. "Gina and I were so worried about the both of you!"

"Any idea when she'll be coming home?" Gina asked.

"Dr. Wilson is thinking I can perhaps bring her home in

a few weeks, providing there's no complications."

"Great," Gina and Wes chimed in unison. Sensing the mood in the room, Harley glanced up at Dan and then at Gina and Wes with her mouth wide open in a smile. Wes patted the couch with his hand, and in a flash Harley jumped into his lap and wagged her tail exuberantly. "Harley is happy to hear this as well," he chuckled. Scratching Harley's head, Gina turned her attention back to Dan. "How are George and Susan doing?"

Dan frowned. "I just talked to George earlier this morning. They're still in the hospital as well. They both underwent surgery and are recovering. Susan was stabbed in her belly and went into labor. The baby also required surgery and is in the neonatal ICU on life support. Trace and I are driving up there to see them this afternoon."

Gina let out a long sigh and looked down at the floor for a few moments. "I hope the baby makes it." She glanced back up at Dan with a puzzled look on her face. "Who's Trace?"

"She's the detective the sheriff called in on the case. Her office is up in Waterton and I need to meet her there in a bit." Peeking up at the clock above the fireplace, he realized he was running a bit late. He was supposed to meet Trace around 1 p.m. and it was already almost 11 a.m. Dan stood up. "Hey guys, I hate to break up our gathering, but I need to get going…"

Wes interrupted Dan's thoughts. "Do they have any suspects yet?"

"Yes, we do have a suspect. I think it's as we suspected all along. This guy, Silas, used to be one of my squad mates, and he's out for revenge."

Gina gasped. "Oh, my God, Dan. Isn't this the guy who

you testified against when he was court-martialed for desertion years ago?"

Dan nodded and reached for his cell to call Trace. He left a message saying he was running late. After ending his call, Dan glanced over at Wes and Gina, and signaled toward the door. He walked over to the coat rack next to the door and pulled on his navy blue down jacket. Gina followed him. Wes shooed Harley off his lap and followed behind Gina as Harley excitedly hurried after his master.

"Dan, I know you need to get going. We do as well. Wes needs to get to work and I need to get back to the computer. Call me when you get a few moments and let's continue our conversation. I hope you and Trace and the sheriff can find this guy and bring him to justice."

"Yeah, me too. I'll call soon."

Wes heartily clapped Dan on the back. "Drive safely and give George and Susan our regards." Dan hugged Wes and Gina and gave Harley another pat on her head. Harley walked her owners through the forest back toward their house. Dan sped off in his Mustang with Trace on his mind.

CHAPTER 13
(Tuesday, March 1, 2016)

Trace paced around outside her office waiting for Dan. It was already after 1 p.m. and she was worried. Glancing at her phone, she noticed the message from Dan letting her know he was running late. A light snow was falling, and she pulled the collar of her navy pea coat closer around her neck as she stood in the parking lot beside her Porsche. *He must be stuck in traffic,* she thought.

Whenever she thought about Dan, she smiled. She was attracted to him, yet she knew in her heart that neither of them were ready for another relationship. She also knew that it wasn't professional to date a client and she chastised herself for even entertaining those thoughts.

Trace and Sheriff Anderson dated for three months, but when she found out about his wife she broke it off. She recalled their first meeting last year when they both attended a conference on Criminology that was held in Waterton. He sat next to her at the conference and they had dinner together the next evening.

Soon thereafter, they became an item. Tom's usual routine was to come over to her house and stay the night, and then return the next day to Archer. Trace hated the long two hour drive to Archer from Waterton, so he always drove up to see her. He tried to keep his marriage a secret from her and did a fairly good job of it, until she made a surprise visit to his home one day. Trace vividly recalled the day and awkward moment, when a woman of medium height and build with sandy brown hair answered the door. She wryly smiled remembering the sheepish look on the sheriff's face when Trace confronted him about "the other woman."

Trace knew in her heart that there was no other woman in Dan's life in light of his present situation, yet thought it best to keep their relationship purely professional.

The sight of Dan's Mustang pulling into the parking lot interrupted her thoughts. Trace ran toward the car and saw Dan get out and walk around to open his passenger side door. Smiling, they greeted each other. "Hey, Detective, sorry I'm late," Dan apologized.

"No worries. I got your message." Dan motioned to the open door. Trace thanked him and got in. Dan slid into the driver's seat and backed his car out of the lot.

"Well, I see that chivalry is still alive after all," she chided.

"Hey, I guess I learned a few things in the Marines." They shared a laugh and headed toward Highway 89 South.

"How far of a drive is it to the hospital?" Trace queried.

"Depending on traffic, it should take around six hours. So, I'll venture a guess that we'll get there around 8 p.m. if we stop for dinner."

"That sounds good. I'm sure we'll be ready to take a dinner break after a long drive."

Dan nodded and they both fell silent for a few minutes and stared out the windows at the cars passing them on Highway 89. Trace broke the silence.

"Hey, how did the funeral ceremony go? Sorry I couldn't be there."

"No worries, Detective. I know you're pretty busy. It went well. My mom flew in from visiting a friend in New York, and it was good seeing and spending time with her. It was just a small family affair with a few neighbors, and Gina did a great job pulling it together. Sheriff Anderson also paid his respects."

Trace tried to keep the conversation focused on Dan.

"It sounds like you and your family are pretty close."

"Yeah, we are. I haven't seen much of mom lately since dad's passing five years ago. I've talked with her often on the phone, but that's about it. We all get along when we're together, especially Gina and I. What's your family situation, Detective?"

"Mom and I are pretty close as well. I don't have any siblings like you do and sometimes I miss that. I have a lot of friends that I keep in touch with, so that fills the void." Trace paused for a few moments deep in thought.

"Speaking of friends, how long has it been since you've seen George?"

"We've talked a few times on the phone, yet the last time I saw him was about five years ago when he and Griffin came up to the Green Mountains to do some downhill skiing."

"So, you're an avid skier?"

"Yeah, I enjoy skiing, although I haven't really had the time as of late due to working long hours at my business…" His voice trailed off. …"well, before this all happened."

Once again Dan fell silent and his eyes filled with tears. A wave of anger washed over him. *It's been over a week since my life was shattered,* he thought, *and I want nothing more than to make Silas pay for the senseless murders of my beloved Peggy and Stephanie.* Trace looked at Dan and felt his anger and sadness. She reached her hand toward him, but instinctively pulled it back. *Remember what you said about keeping this relationship professional,* she admonished herself.

"Dan…" Trace paused and searched for the right words to say to him. "I know how it feels to lose someone you love." Dan glanced over at Trace and their eyes met. "So, what's your story, Detective?"

Trace let out a long sigh and stared out the window for a few seconds. She noticed it was now snowing harder and that Dan had turned on the windshield wipers.

Suddenly her mind was immersed in memories of Ron, her partner when she worked as a police officer. The images of that nightmarish summer evening three years ago were as fresh and vivid as though they happened just yesterday.

She was back again with Ron on that fateful summer evening, when they were riding pretty fast on his motorcycle on a hilly, winding road. She recalled them speeding around tight curves, and she realized they were definitely going too fast for the conditions. It all happened so fast! She could hear herself yelling at him to slow down, yet before she finished her sentence, the car darted out in front of them from a side street. Ron slammed on the brakes, but he still wasn't able to stop in time. She vividly remembered how they were both thrown from the cycle. She heard a thud, and out of her peripheral vision she saw Ron land in a crumpled heap on the ground.

She was catapulted through the air and landed in a clump of bushes mere inches from a long drop off down to the coastline below. She heard herself screaming as she fell. Clutching at a protruding tree branch for all she was worth, the branch broke her fall. As she hung by her hands from the tree branch, she glanced down at the waves splashing on the beach below and felt sick to her stomach. Slowly and arduously, she climbed up the tree branch and finally managed to swing both legs back up to the edge of the road.

She sat for a few moments on the side of the road trying to catch her breath and calm herself. Wiping tears from her face, she noticed she had blood on her hands and several deep lacerations on both legs. With Ron on her mind, she raced back down the road to him surrounded by paramedics, and saw his motionless body lying in a pool of blood.

Trace bit her lip in an attempt to keep from crying, yet the tears now streamed down her cheeks. She brushed her coat sleeve over her face and quickly wiped the tears away. Dan glanced over at her and studied her face for a few seconds. "Are you okay?" he quietly asked.

She shook her head, fighting back the tears and tried to find the words to portray the anguish and grief she felt at that moment.

"When I was working as a police officer, I used to ride with my partner, this guy named Ron. He was my partner for two of the three years I worked in the police force. At that time, I lived and worked in New Hampshire where I was born. We were dating on the side and we fell in love."

Trace let out another sigh and paused for a few seconds to regain her composure as she relived the painful memories. "In a matter of seconds, like you, my happy life was shattered. We were riding on his motorcycle one beautiful evening and got into an accident. Ron sustained major head and other injuries and never regained consciousness. He died in the ambulance before reaching the hospital."

Both were silent for a few moments until Dan spoke. "Trace, I'm sorry for your loss." He kept his eyes focused on the highway lost in his own thoughts. Fighting to hold back more tears, Dan's last words came into her mind. *That's strange that Dan called me Trace. He always called me Detective.*

"Thanks, Corporal," she whispered.

Dan briefly glanced at her and smiled.

"Corporal? That was a long time ago, Detective. You must have done your homework."

Trace remembered she promised to give Dan the lab and autopsy reports. "Yes, and by the way, the blood types found on the knife match that of your wife and daughters. We're still waiting for the results of all the crime scene reports. Just FYI, results can often take up to a month or more."

"I figured as much."

They both fell silent and stared out the window. The snow was still falling hard, and as it got darker and colder, the highway got slicker. Dan felt his car fishtail several times and noticed he was "white-knuckling" the steering wheel. The dashboard clock flashed 5 p.m. at him.

He observed another flashing sign ahead that read "Gas, Food and Lodging" along Highway 95, the road on which they were driving. Trace also noticed the sign and excitedly asked, "Hey, are you hungry? I know this great restaurant called Sandie's. I'm pretty familiar with the Portsmouth area and Sandie's has great food." Dan nodded and pulled into the gas station to fill up his tank. Afterward, they drove around the corner from the gas station to Sandie's.

They got out of the car, hurried into the restaurant, and were greeted by the hostess, a short, heavyset woman. Smiling at them she asked, "Just the two of you?" Dan nodded and replied, "Yes, a booth please, if you have one available." They followed the hostess to a booth near the back of the restaurant by a window. Dan helped Trace remove her coat and hung it on the coat rack behind their booth. She sat down as the hostess handed their menus to her. "Your waitress will be right with you." Thanking her, Dan watched her walk down the aisle toward the front of the restaurant. Looking back at Trace, he held up his hand. "I'll be right back," he replied.

Trace noticed he walked toward the hostess and started a conversation with her. *Wonder what they're talking about,* she pondered. She glanced at the menu and decided she was hungry enough to order more than just a salad. Dan soon returned and sat down across from her at their booth. "It's getting kind of late. The hostess told me there's a motel also called Sandie's right down the block and we could stay there for the night if you'd like."

"Sure, that's fine. We're in New Hampshire, but still at least two hours away from Lakeland. We could get an early start in the morning when we're more rested."

"Yeah, it's still snowing pretty good, and hopefully the plows will clear the roads tomorrow so driving won't be too bad." Trace handed Dan a menu, and studied him as he studied the menu with a puzzled look on his face.

Smiling, she leaned forward toward him. "If you're into seafood, I highly recommend the seafood stew. It's yummy." Peering over the top of the menu at Trace, he smiled and shook his head. "Okay, Detective, that sounds delicious, yet I've got more of a taste for steak."

"I'm going for the seafood."

"Okay, so be it."

The waitress came over to their booth, took their orders, and rushed down the aisle toward the kitchen area near the back of the restaurant. Trace looked around the restaurant and thought it looked more modern than when she was last there a few years ago visiting her mom. The wooden floors were a deep wooden brown, as were the chairs and bar, and in the middle of the restaurant there was a white brick fireplace with brown trim. The atmosphere was still rustic with a quaint New England charm all its own.

The restaurant tables were filled with people, yet Trace and Dan enjoyed being some distance away from the main section of the restaurant to afford them a bit of privacy. Sandie's brought back fond memories of when Ron proposed to her there over three years prior. Dan's voice brought her back to the present. "You look thoughtful, Detective."

Returning his gaze, she replied, "Oh, yeah, sorry about that. Took a detour down memory lane." The waitress brought them two glasses of red wine and then hurried toward another table. As they held up their glasses, Trace announced,

"So, here's to us bringing Silas to justice." They touched glasses together in a toast and sipped their wine.

"So, tell me, Detective, you mentioned you were living and working as a police officer in this area. How long did you live here?"

"I was born right here in this town, Portsmouth. My mom is elderly and lives here alone just outside of town. I visit every few weeks or so to check in on her. So far, mom's doing well. She manages to keep active by spending lots of time in her garden and it keeps her young." Trace smiled.

"What about your dad?"

Her smile faded into a frown. "Dad passed away almost two years ago from a severe infection in his leg. He served as an infantry soldier in Vietnam from '68 through '72, and was wounded in action and lost a leg. He was decorated with a Purple Heart. He and mom met in '78 and married in '80. Three years later, I was born."

"Were you and he fairly close?"

Trace sighed. "Yes, he was truly a very brave man, and inspired me to serve my country as a law enforcement officer."

Dan stared at Trace with a slight smile on his face.

"The apple never falls far from the tree."

Blushing, she lowered her eyes for a few moments, then met his gaze. "Thanks. So, enough about me. What about your family?"

Dan looked thoughtful. "My dad was also in the military. He served as a Staff Sergeant in active combat in the Korean War from '50 to '53. Because of his service, I joined the Marines. He passed away in 2011 and mom and I took it pretty hard."

Dan studied Trace's face and as if reading her mind, replied, "In answer to your next question, yes, I miss dad a lot. He and I spent a considerable amount of time together playing baseball when I was a kid, and he taught me a lot about architecture and life in general when I got older. I took over his architecture business after he passed. Mom and I do okay, but we sometimes don't see eye to eye about things. Gina, my sister, and mom, get along pretty well. Since this happened to Peggy and the girls, I've been living in a cabin that my dad built and I have fond memories there of his living years." Dan chuckled as he recalled and told Trace the story about when he and his dad were working on the cabin and Dan hit his thumb with the hammer instead of the nail he was aiming for. His dad held up his nail gun, patted Dan on the shoulder, and wryly announced, "These guns get the job done, son, and spare the hands."

Dinner finally arrived and they hungrily ate and spent the next few hours getting to know each other, laughing and enjoying each other's company.

After dinner, they enjoyed a delicious dessert of Key lime pie, and feeling tired, they decided to call it a night. Trace looked out the window and noticed only a light sprinkling of wet snow falling.

When the waitress brought their bill, Trace reached for it, yet Dan was quicker. "My treat, Detective." Once again, Dan's hand brushed against hers sending small tingles up her spine. *This guy is your client for God's sake, and his wife and daughter were just murdered,* her inner critic warned.

After paying the bill, Dan brought her coat down from the rack and carefully wrapped it around her shoulders. She thanked him and momentarily gazed into his eyes. She noticed a similar tenderness in his eyes that she observed when he was in her office with the sheriff.

They left the restaurant and walked out to Dan's snow-covered Mustang. Once again, he opened her passenger side door, then walked around and slid into the driver's seat. They drove down the block to the motel and parked in the back lot.

As they walked around to the front of the motel, Dan once again fell silent and recalled times of the recent past when he walked hand in hand with Peggy. *How I miss her and Stephanie, yet there's something about Trace that's appealing. She's suffered through her grief and makes me momentarily forget my own.*

Trace was also deep in thought about Dan. She felt a tug of war going on inside her brain. The rational part was pulling her toward her mom's house just a few miles outside of town, yet her heart told her not to be so rational. *She longed to feel his strong arms around her and feel his body next to hers… STOP IT,* she scolded herself. *NOT HERE, NOT NOW!*

"Dan, I… I need to check in on my mom, since we're so close to her house. We could stay there for the night, and you can sleep in the guest bedroom. She's all alone…"

"It's okay, Detective. I understand." Their eyes locked as they stood face to face. "Let's go," he suddenly said with an urgency in his voice. "It's getting pretty cold out here." Trace nodded and they silently walked back to his car. As they drove toward the house, Trace called her mom and told her they would arrive within the next fifteen minutes.

Leona Malone, a petite, grey-haired lady in her 60's met them at the door.

They entered the rustic two story farmhouse and Trace and her mom hugged for a few moments. Dan stood in the doorway watching their interaction. "Mom, this is Dan, a client of mine. Dan, this is my mom." Leona smiled at Dan and they shook hands. "Dan, so nice to meet you!" She patted his hand. "Please come in and have a seat," she signaled toward the couch. Trace walked over to the couch and sat down. Dan followed behind Trace.

From behind him he heard Leona ask, "May I take your coat?"

Dan shook his head and sat down next to Trace on the couch. "No thanks, ma'am. I'll just keep it on for a while." Leona smiled at Dan. "Yeah, it's pretty cold out there. At least it stopped snowing." Leona sat in her recliner across from Trace and Dan and observed they were sitting close to each other.

Trace was the first to speak. "Sorry to get here so late, but we had a lot to discuss at dinner and on our way up here."

Leona waved a dismissive hand at her daughter and laughed. "Oh, think nothing of it, my dear. I know you have a pretty crazy schedule. I would offer you something to eat and drink, yet you guys already ate."

Dan glanced around the living room where they sat and noticed the cozy, homey atmosphere and lingering smell of some freshly baked pie. The clock on the wall above the TV next to Leona's recliner chimed at the stroke of 10 p.m. The TV was on in the background promoting some new diet pills on the market to "help you lose weight fast…" Sinking back into the comfy buttercup yellow couch pillows, Dan felt his body start to relax. Trace and her mom were engaged in conversation so he momentarily closed his eyes.

For a few minutes, he listened to a commercial droning on and started to snooze. The sound of the news suddenly hit him in the gut. "Waterton police are still looking for this man, Silas Samuels, in connection with another attack on two more victims…" Dan and Trace both stared intently at the pictures that flashed across the screen. The first was a pencil drawing of the murder suspect who bore a striking resemblance to someone they both knew too well. The second showed pictures of Jennie Andrews and her boyfriend, Sean Johnson.

Trace and Dan's eyes locked, and Trace was suddenly on her feet. "That's the convenience store girl I told you about. I was pulling into the parking lot and Silas was pulling out."

Dan stood up and nervously ran his fingers through his hair. "We need to find Silas, Trace, and it can't happen fast enough," he replied with great urgency in his voice. "I need to contact Griffin and Nielson…"

Trace stared at Dan as he walked toward the door.

"Where are you going?" Trace asked. Leona suddenly interjected. "Wait a minute, you guys. What's going on?"

Trace looked at Leona who was now standing next to her with a puzzled expression on her face. "Mom, I'll fill you in, I promise." Turning back toward Dan, she followed him to the door. "Dan… don't leave…" she begged and reached for his arm.

Dan's eyes once again met hers. "I'll be back tomorrow, Detective. I'm going back to the motel down the road to make a few phone calls. What time do you want me to pick you up?"

"Okay… I'll call you tomorrow morning."

Dan nodded to Trace and then to Leona.

"Thanks, ma'am for your kind hospitality. I'll let you

two have some quality time together."

"Dan, if you change your mind, we'll be up for a while. Please know you are always welcome to stay." Thanking her, he smiled and shook her hand, and walked out the door.

Mother and daughter watched Dan walk to his car and drive back down the road toward Sandie's Motel. They walked back to the couch and sat down.

Leona studied her daughter's face for some answers. Trace sheepishly cast a sidelong glance at her mom. Gently patting her daughter's hand, she remarked, "Okay, so correct me if I'm wrong. You've got a thing going on between the two of you. What have you gotten yourself into now?"

Trace wearily shook her head. "It's been a long day, mom, yet I kept it professional." Letting out a long sigh, she informed her mom about the events of the past week.

Leona stared in shocked disbelief at her daughter after hearing her heart-rending tale.

CHAPTER 14
(Tuesday March 1, 2016)

Silas was on a mission. Packing his knife in his brief-case, he hurried out the door of his motel room. He checked out of the motel and hurried down the street toward Jose's Garage.

He took a quick look at his watch and noted it was 2:05 p.m. He had spent the morning eating an early breakfast at the motel and watching the news. They were still showing that bad pencil drawing of him, yet they now knew his name. *Good thing I'm getting a new ID and car remodeling. They'll never find me now,* he scornfully smiled at the thought.

Feeling hungry, he stopped outside of Hank's and considered running inside for a quick burger and to see if the waitress was working today. He peered through the window and saw the same two cops sitting inside and decided to forgo the burger and waitress. Silas turned away and headed toward Jose's Garage, unaware that one of the officers caught a glance of him staring through the window.

Officer Murray stopped his conversation with his partner, Officer Ramsey, and nodded toward the window where Silas stood just moments before. Looking down at his cell, he accessed the pencil sketch drawing from the newscasts and showed the photo to his partner. "That guy looks a lot like our perp, minus the facial hair," he remarked to Ramsey.

"I didn't get a good look at him. Just caught a brief glimpse of a black trench coat…"

"Let's go," Murray interjected. He signaled the waitress for the check, and they quickly exited Hank's in pursuit of the guy with the trench coat.

As Silas hurried down the street toward Jose's, he had the strange feeling someone was following him. Glancing behind him, he noticed the two cops were leaving Hank's and getting into their squad car. He quickly entered a curio shop a few doors down from Jose's and hurried to the back of the store. The short, dark-haired lady behind the counter, surprised by Silas' sudden entrance, stared up from her desk, and asked if he needed any help. Silas shook his head and remarked, "No thanks, just looking." He pretended to be interested in the scores of colorful, hand painted jewelry, figurines, and trinkets lining the many shelves of the shop.

The counter lady watched him make his way over toward a rack of clothing with his back toward her. She felt a strange aura about him that made her suspicious.

Glancing up to the wall behind her counter at the poster of a man wanted by the Waterton Police, she instantly made the connection. Remembering the phone in the back room, she slowly walked in that direction. "Sir, I'll be back in a few minutes," she remarked to Silas still standing with his back toward her. Slipping into the back room, she locked the door behind her, ran to the phone and dialed 911. "What's your emergency?" she heard the voice ask over the phone.

Lowering her voice, she shakily replied, "There's a man here wearing a black trench coat that I believe is wanted by the police. Please come quickly…" she begged and gave them her address.

She heard a noise outside the door and it sounded like the front door of her store opening and closing. Hoping it was the police, she nervously bit her lip and held her breath and listened.

The next thing she heard was the heavy thud of someone crashing through the locked back room door. Gasping in terror at the man in the trench coat running at her, she screamed and fled toward the back door of her shop. She flung open the door, but before she could run out, Silas tackled her to the ground. Lying on her belly, she tried to scream. She felt Silas' gloved hand cover her mouth to muffle her scream. She tried to bite his hand, but he quickly pulled his hand away and wrapped duct tape around her mouth and head. With her one free hand she landed a backward punch to his head. Silas flipped her onto her back and delivered a fierce punch to her face.

With tears and blood dripping down her face, she fought to stay conscious and forced herself to concentrate on the details of his face. The hideous gleeful smile and sinister eyes filled with hatred made her heart feel like it was pounding right out of her chest. She heard the ominous tone of his voice booming in her ear. "One false move and you're dead, sweetheart."

She felt her hands and feet being bound with duct tape. He dragged her squirming body toward the chair she once sat on and he pushed her down into the chair. She momentarily fainted as her hands and feet were being tied to the back of the chair.

After a few minutes, she regained consciousness and found herself face to face with an angry Silas. He pulled his gun from his holster and pointed the gun at her head. "You ratted on me," he angrily yelled at her. She felt his hot, rancid breath on her face and felt faint once again.

The sound of sirens interrupted his rant. Silas ran into the main part of the store and stopped by a rack of old clothing. Picking out an old camouflage army jacket and baseball hat, he donned them and hung up his trench coat on the empty hanger. He ran toward the back door and out the door into the alley behind the store. Seeing two squad cars parked in the alley, he ran back into the back room, through the store, and out the front door.

Silas quickly looked around him as he hurried toward Jose's, and noticed the street was filled with people hustling to their destinations. He became aware of two officers walking toward him heading toward the Curio Shop. He turned his head away from them and pulled his cap down over his eyes. When the officers passed, he breathed a sigh of relief. *She'll keep them busy for a while,* he thought.

Approaching Jose's, he noticed a tall, lanky, balding figure standing outside and recognized it was Tony standing by a newly painted silver Camaro. Tony greeted Silas as he approached him. "I thought you might need this ready," he dryly smiled and handed Silas the keys. "You better hurry, man. The fuzz are onto someone right now and I'm taking a wild guess it's you!"

"Thanks, Tony. No time for pleasantries. Gotta run."

Silas grabbed the keys from Tony, threw his briefcase on the back seat and got into his new vehicle. Tony signaled to Silas as he rolled down the window. "You might also need this, Mr. Wyatt," he sneered and handed Silas the false ID. Smiling, Silas reached for the ID then sped down the street toward Highway 7 South, yelling out the window, "Say hey to Jose!"

Jackie Hugo, the curio shop owner, grimaced in pain as Officer Murray carefully removed the tape from her mouth, hands and feet. "Thank you," she whispered. She tearfully recounted all the details she could recall of her ordeal to the officer.

Jackie paused for a few moments to regain her composure and wipe her face with her shirtsleeve. Officer Murray, a tall and muscular man with light brown hair, handed her a handkerchief he pulled from his pocket. Jackie gratefully accepted the hanky and held it over her bloody nose. She glanced over at Officer Ramsey, a shorter, sandy-haired man, who stood guard by the back door while several officers patrolled the store and its outside perimeter.

While they waited for the paramedics to arrive, Officer Murray continued his interrogation. "Jackie, can you give me a description of this guy?"

Jackie slowly nodded. "Yes. He's pretty muscular, and is medium in height, with dark brown wavy hair and the start of a beard. He was carrying a briefcase. His eyes were the most hateful eyes I've ever seen."

"Did you notice if he had any weapons?"

"Yes, he was holding a gun to my head until he heard your sirens and ran out the back door." She paused for a few moments trying to recall more details about her assailant. "He ran back into this room when he saw your squad cars…" her voice suddenly trailed off. Sirens from an approaching ambulance were heard outside and soon two paramedics were walking in the front of the store. An officer directed them to the back room.

"Jackie, I have more questions for another time. We'll stay in touch and let you know of any further developments. I'm sure these guys will take good care of you." Murray nodded at her and left the room.

She thanked him and feeling faint, almost fell off her chair. The paramedics rushed toward Jackie and helped her onto a gurney. As they wheeled her outside, Murray did a final walk through the store. He signaled to Ramsey who followed him. They walked past the rack of clothing when Murray quickly stopped at the sound of Ramsey's voice calling to him. He turned around and saw Ramsey holding a black trench coat in front of him.

Silas peered out his rear view mirror as he drove onto the ramp leading to Highway 7 South. He didn't see any cops following him and breathed a sigh of relief. Removing his cap, he ran his arm along his forehead and wiped off beads of sweat. As he drove into the rapidly descending dusk, his mind was flooded with thoughts. He thought about the lady at the curio shop with a sardonic smile on his face. *She deserved the punch for ratting on me,* he thought. *She could have gotten off a lot worse, but she was lucky the cops came when they did. She could've given the cops a description of me, but they'll be looking for Silas, who no longer exists.* He laughed aloud as he remembered Tony called him Mr. Wyatt.

He reached into his army jacket pocket and pulled out the fake ID and looked at the name on the card. It read Stuart Wyatt with a fake Waterton address, and showed the same old picture he used as Silas. Slipping the ID back into his pocket, he repeated the name several times. "That name has a ring to it. I like it!"

He turned on the radio to his favorite music station, and heard the news blaring out at him. "Thanks for listening to radio station 95 Triple X, and now for the 5 o'clock news. "The East Coast Killer has claimed another victim. Jackie Hugo, who owns the curio shop in Waterton, was assaulted while in her shop earlier this afternoon. She was treated for minor facial injuries and a nose fracture at Waterton Memorial Hospital and released. Officers Murray and Ramsey spotted the killer peeking into Hank's Hamburgers restaurant and pursued him, yet were unable to apprehend him. Waterton Police are questioning all business owners in town for any information on Silas Samuels, an ex-Marine, and are warning that this man is armed and dangerous. The only clue they have so far is a black trench coat found at the crime scene left by Samuels…"

Silas reached up to turn off the radio and frowned. He recalled when his mother gave his dad the coat as a birthday present. His dad never wore it. *Bastard!* He stole the coat from his dad when he finally left that hell hole when he enlisted in the Marines in his early twenties, and wore it ever since. *I hated to give it up,* he thought, *but maybe it's for the best that I don't have to keep being reminded of HIM!*

The more he thought about his dad, the angrier he felt. *I hate the man, hate everything he stands for, the constant drinking, the beatings. I hate what he did to me!*

"BASTARD!" he yelled and accelerated down the highway toward his childhood home in Pines, Pennsylvania where his hateful dad still lived.

CHAPTER 15
(Wednesday, March 2, 2016)

Trace winced at the ringtone sound of her cell that woke her from a sound sleep at 7 a.m. Reaching for her phone on the nightstand next to her bed, she groggily answered.

"Did I wake you, Detective?" Hearing Dan's voice made her smile.

"Yes, but thanks for waking me up. I need to get up and get moving. We have places to go and people to see." Trace yawned and now Dan was smiling.

"It sounds like you and mom were partying last night."

"We stayed up past midnight. Mom's a party animal."

"What about her daughter?"

"Every time we get together, we try to solve the world's problems." *We mostly talked about you,* she wanted to tell him.

"Did you come up with any solutions?"

"Yeah, all the world's problems were solved in one

night." They laughed. After a few moments, Trace asked, "Did you get any sleep?"

"A few hours. I was able to connect with Griffin. I woke him up also."

Trace glanced at the clock on the wall of her bedroom and saw it was already 7:20 a.m. "Hey, I need to get moving here. Let's chat more in the car. I want to hear about Griffin. See you in about an hour."

Trace hung up the phone and rummaged around in her overnight bag for a pair of sweatpants. Remembering that they would be meeting George and Susan, she threw the sweats back into her bag, and pulled out a more professional looking navy blue pantsuit and white lace blouse. She quickly dressed, applied light makeup, and pulled her hair back in a ponytail. Satisfied with her appearance, she hurried downstairs.

Before entering the kitchen, she glanced down the hallway toward her mom's bedroom and saw the door was still closed. She remembered her mom told her to wake her up before she left with Dan, yet she decided it was best to let her sleep. *This wasn't the best time to engage in any lengthy conversation like they always did,* she thought.

She made some coffee and grabbed a carton of yogurt from the fridge. Walking over to the dining room table, she saw a pad of paper laying on the table and wrote a note to her mom.

Hey Mom,

Sorry I missed you. Dan picked me up early.

Thanks for your great insights and conversation last night. I'll be in touch.

Love always,

Trace

As she sipped her coffee, she thought about Dan and remembered their phone conversation. He remarked about contacting Griffin. She wondered how he reacted to what Dan told him about Silas.

Just as she spooned some yogurt into her mouth, there was a knock at the door. Trace ran to the door and Dan walked in and greeted her with a smile.

"Good morning, Detective. Ready?"

"Almost. Just have to grab my coffee and yogurt, and we're on the road." Watching her rush around the dining room, he asked, "That's all you're eating?"

Trace gave him a sidelong glance as she grabbed her tote bag on the table next to her coffee and yogurt. "Yeah, that's my breakfast of choice. Was yours any better?"

Dan laughed. "Hey, my sweet roll and French toast is more substantial than what you're eating." He patted his stomach.

"Okay, if you say so." Smiling, she walked to her coat draped over the couch in the front room. Dan followed and helped her don her coat.

Dan looked around the room and down the hall. "So, I guess mom is still sleeping off her rough night."

She put her finger to her lips and quietly walked into the dining room to gather her breakfast items. "Let's go before she wakes up," she whispered.

Dan opened the door and walked outside. Trace followed and locked the door behind her.

The sun was shining as they continued their drive up to Lakeland. They started out around 8:45 a.m. and Trace figured they would reach the hospital without stops by noon.

The hours flew by as they conversed and drove North on highway 95 along the scenic Atlantic coastline, its blackened waters crashing into the shoreline.

Dan talked about his conversation with Griffin and George. He remembered Griffin's comments as he filled him in on Silas' attacks on George and Susan as well as his own.

"We stayed up pretty late as well and had a lot to talk about. He already knew about Silas' attacks from the news."

"Did he recognize Silas?"

Dan nodded. "He said he recognized his picture, and vividly recalled his court-martial and dishonorable discharge. I remember his last words, that he would notify the Adirondacks Police about Silas' plans, and how their SWAT team would be ready to give him a "hero's welcome." He smiled at the thought.

Both Dan and Trace were quiet, lost in their own thoughts for most of the drive. Dan was looking forward to seeing George again after so many years, but was also overwhelmed with hospital visits. He didn't want to see another friend of his hurt by Silas' quest for blood and vengeance. He also missed seeing Annie and had wanted to call the night before, but figured it was late and she was probably sleeping.

Trace was pondering questions she wanted to ask George and Susan, and wondered about how their baby was doing. Suddenly, Annie came to mind.

Their dual dialogue was simultaneously verbalized.

"How's…" Trace started to ask.

"Annie?" Dan looked at her with a smile, yet Trace could detect a hint of sadness in his eyes. "I never thought you would ask, Detective." She's hanging in there. Dr. Wilson called last night and said she's still pretty weak and coughing a lot. Dr. Wilson said she's still wearing an oxygen mask and he's concerned about the possibility of complications like pneumonia.'"

"Does he know how much longer she needs to stay in the hospital?" Trace sipped her coffee and scraped the last yogurt remnants into her mouth with her finger.

"He's thinking at least another few weeks."

Dan shook his head deep in thought. *I wish I were there with you Annie. Miss you, sweetheart, and I'm sure you miss me, too.*

Dan saw they were driving through town so he turned on his GPS. They soon arrived at Penobscot County Hospital and Dan pulled into the parking lot. He called George to let him know they arrived.

Trace started to open her door and this time Dan didn't rush to open it for her. They silently walked together through the main entrance and headed toward the check-in desk.

After asking the receptionist for the room number for George, they took the elevator to the sixth floor. When the elevator door opened, a tall, sandy-haired man standing by the nurse's desk was waiting for them. He had an IV in one hand and held onto an IV pole with the other.

Recognizing Dan approaching him, George smiled and extended his free arm toward Dan.

"Hey, Corporal. Long time, no see," George greeted Dan and they hugged and clapped each other's backs.

"Hey, Sergeant. You're looking great for someone who's supposed to be on death's doorknob," Dan teased.

"Not there quite yet so don't rush the process," George razzed him back.

Trace stood behind Dan for a few moments as she watched the two men interact. Clearing her throat, Trace stepped forward and Dan introduced her to George.

"This is Detective Trace Malone. Trace, George Adams."

"Nice to meet you, Detective," George declared. Trace took note of a similar formal greeting that Dan used to address her. *Dan had a slightly different, kinder tone.*

"Same here, Sergeant." After shaking hands, they all walked down the hall to George's room. George sat on the side of his bed and pulled the two sides of his hospital gown together behind him. He signaled for Trace and Dan to sit on the two chairs next to his bed. They looked around and noticed it was a typical hospital room: sparse and functional. They sat down on chairs with the covers worn and frayed in the corners.

They exchanged small talk about the weather and their trip from Waterton. After a few moments, Trace changed the subject.

"So, Sergeant, I have many questions for you."

George nodded. "I'm sure you do, Detective. Ask away. And please call me George."

"First and foremost, how are you feeling? How are Susan and the baby?"

"I'm doing pretty well under the circumstances. Still have a few rough edges, but can't complain." He lifted one corner of his gown to reveal a huge surgical dressing wrapped around his midsection. Trace also noticed a large dressing covering his left thigh. After a few moments, George continued. "As for Susan, she's been in ICU, then the OB department for observation since delivering the baby a few days ago. She knows you two are here today and she'll be down in a bit."

Dan leaned forward in his chair toward George. "How's the baby?"

George let out a long sigh. "She's still in NICU on life support and we don't know if she'll make it or not..." his voice trailed off and his eyes welled up with tears. "Dr. Smith told us that our little Lynette has a collapsed lung and rib fracture. He said she has a fair chance to recover provided there are no complications like pneumonia. So, we're taking it day to day."

Dan got up from his chair and patted George on the shoulder. "Hey, old buddy, I know how you're feeling." George slowly stood up to face Dan and clapped him on his back. "Sorry to hear about Peggy and Stephanie." Trace noticed Dan was also teary-eyed.

After a few moments of silence, Dan found his voice. "Thanks, man." They warmly embraced.

Susan stood outside the room taking in the scene before making her entrance. Trace noticed a pale, slender woman slowly enter the room. She had long brown hair hanging down to her shoulders and she walked with a walker for support. Trace stood up and walked over to her. "You must be Susan," Trace greeted her. Susan tried to smile yet was in obvious pain.

"And you must be Detective Malone." After shaking hands with Trace and Dan, Trace offered Susan her seat, but she politely declined the offer. She turned toward the bed where George was now seated and sat down next to him. He smiled at her and they held hands. Seeing that Susan was settled, Trace and Dan sat back down in their chairs.

Susan was the first to speak. "Thank you, Dan and

Detective Malone, for coming today all the way from Waterton. That was very kind of you." She coyly smiled and blushed.

Dan pensively glanced at Susan. "You're very welcome. We heard about your situation on the news, and of course, we knew we had to come and visit. We're so sorry to hear about your baby."

Susan stared at Dan, her eyes wet with tears. "Thank you." She paused for a few seconds, barely able to contain her emotions, and wiped her eyes with a tissue she pulled from her bathrobe pocket. George squeezed her hand and they exchanged glances.

"I'm sure George has already shared our deepest condolences for your wife and daughters. Is there any further news about this lunatic or his whereabouts?"

Trace leaned forward in her chair. "We have a definite suspect and have every reason to believe our suspect was a member of Dan's and George's squadron." Trace directed her next question to George. "Does the name Silas Samuels sound familiar?"

George now stared intently at Dan. "Yeah… I remember him well. He's the deserter guy I ran after and saved his damn worthless life!"

Dan solemnly nodded. "That's him."

"When I talked with Detective Randolph from the Lakeland Police Department a few days ago, he questioned me about any details I could remember about this guy. I was still pretty out of it from the anesthesia, yet recalled the dog tags around his neck. After Randolph left, I thought about each of our squadron mates, and figured it was Silas. He's the only guy that has a motive for revenge."

Glancing at Trace, Susan asked, "Are you guys aware of his other victims? We just saw on the news last night that Silas' latest victim was the owner of a curio shop in Waterton. I think her name is Jackie something or other…"

Trace interrupted her. "Jackie Hugo. I was just in her store a few weeks ago. I wonder why he would attack her? What's his motivation there?" she wondered aloud.

Dan glanced at Trace and replied, "I think she was just in the wrong place at the wrong time. We might have an idea of his current whereabouts." Trace pulled out her notepad and pen from her coat pocket and jotted down some notes. Trace looked up at Dan. "True, we have an idea, yet he most likely has fled the area by now. I know the officers at Waterton PD. I will contact them for more details."

Trace turned her focus to Susan and George. "I also had an encounter with Silas." She described the night at the convenience store in Waterton and how she followed Silas to the house of the store clerk and all that transpired afterward.

Susan and George listened, transfixed at her story.

"… I almost caught him, but he made a quick getaway through the window…" She paused for a few moments and declared, "We will catch him!"

Dan looked over at Trace and noticed her serious expression and tone of voice.

The lunch cart appeared in the hallway. George smiled and asked Trace and Dan, "Have you guys had lunch yet? I can ask for a few guest trays if you wish."

Dan and Trace exchanged glances. Dan spoke first. "Thanks for your kind offer, but we'll probably stop somewhere to grab a bite on our way back to Waterton. We should get going soon anyway and let you eat."

Dan glanced at Trace. "Any more questions, Detective?"

"Yes, actually. I have one more question and then you can enjoy your lunch." She directed her question to George. "I was wondering since you and Dan spent a lot of time together with Silas in your squadron, do you know anything about his family history?"

George thought for a few moments. "Not really. He didn't really mention his family to me. Wait a minute... on one occasion he and I had a discussion about why we joined the Marines and he told me he joined to get away from his dad. Other than that, he didn't tell me anything further. I just assumed his dad was a bit overbearing like some dads can be. Sorry I'm not more helpful."

"Well, okay. So, this leads to a few more questions. What prompted you to join the Marines?"

"My dad served in the Marines and I followed suit, similar to Dan. He never forced me to join. When I was a boy, I remember seeing him in uniform with all his medals. I wanted to be just like him."

Dan smiled at George and proclaimed, "Mission accomplished. Your dad would be proud." George nodded at Dan. "Thanks, yours as well."

Dan stared down at the floor as he felt the familiar melancholy mood settle in whenever he thought of his father. He pondered George's comment about Silas and his dad and was willing to place bets that their relationship wasn't close.

Trace jotted down a few notes, and feeling hunger pangs gnawing at her stomach, she stood up from her chair. "Thanks so much, George and Susan. That's all I have for now.

I wish you both speedy recoveries, and prayers for baby Lynette."

She and Dan walked over to the bed and shook hands with them. Leaning down toward George, she met his gaze and replied, "You've been more helpful than you know." Patting his shoulder, she glanced over at Dan standing next to her and they both left the room. Glancing behind her, Trace saw George and Susan ravenously consuming the contents of their lunch trays. When they passed the lunch cart, she smelled the food and felt like doing the same.

Shortly after Dan and Trace left the room, someone was rushing toward the room and bumped into Dan. He stared at the short, stocky man wearing a tan trench coat and black derby who almost knocked him over. "Sorry sir. I didn't mean to crash into you. My mind was somewhere else. Were you visiting Mr. Adams?"

Dan nodded. "Yes, I'm a friend of George's. We served together in the Marines." The man reached in his coat pocket and flashed his badge at them. "Detective Mike Randolph. I'm working with Mr. and Mrs. Adams on this case." He turned toward Dan and shook his hand. "I thought I recognized you from the picture Mr. Adams showed me. Sorry about your wife and daughters."

Turning toward Trace, he shook her hand. "And you must be Detective Malone. I know you're working with Waterton PD on this case as well. I've been in contact with a few officers from WPD. We should talk sometime and compare notes." He pulled out some business cards and handed them his cards. Reaching for the card, Trace replied, "Yes, I would like to find out what information you have gathered on this case, and I'll be in touch." They all shook hands and Randolph headed into George's room. Trace and Dan walked down the corridor toward the elevator.

As they left the hospital, Dan turned toward Trace.

"Okay, Detective. Are you still hungry?"

Trace rolled her eyes. "Hell, yeah!"

Dan looked across the street and spotted a small restaurant called Dino's. They started crossing the street, but stopped long enough to allow a screaming ambulance race by them. Dan exclaimed, "Great, just what we need right now, more excitement, right?" Trace smiled and nodded. "Yeah, like a hole in the head!"

They both laughed away all the tension of the day along their walk to Dino's. When they arrived at Dino's, a small Italian restaurant, they were seated at a secluded table for two. The restaurant smelled of sinfully delicious tomato sauce and had a bar and wide screen TV on the wall behind the bar. From the TV, strains of a hockey game in progress were heard amidst cheers from the audience. They ordered a large sausage and mushroom pizza to share. While waiting for their pizza, they sipped on lemonades.

Trace gazed at Dan and sighed. "You know, I shouldn't be drinking while on duty."

"Come on, Detective. You're off duty now, right?"

Trace met his gaze and smiled. "Yeah, guess so."

Dan suddenly became quiet and stared at the black and white checkered floor tile. Trace studied his face and felt his sadness.

"A penny for your thoughts."

Dan's eyes once again met hers. "Nothing special. Just

thinking…" his voice trailed off and cracked.

"About Peggy?" Trace bit her lip and felt guilty for going there.

Dan paused for a few moments, deep in thought. He slowly nodded and his eyes were wet with tears.

"Our first date was at a pizza parlor." We shared the same pizza, just like we're doing." He managed to smile, yet Trace could still see and feel his sadness.

"Where did you two meet?

"We went to the same college, good old U of A. I was one year ahead. She was working on her teaching degree and I was studying business administration. We met in the study hall, and the rest is history. I guess you could say it was love at first sight… once again his voice trailed off.

"I know this is painful, Dan. If you don't want to talk about this, I understand."

The waitress brought their pizza and for the next hour they ate and laughed and momentarily forgot theirs and the world's problems.

After finishing lunch, Dan became quiet again.

Trace lowered her voice to almost a whisper. "I understand how you feel. There are times I really miss Ron, and yes, it sucks, but believe me when I say that it really does get easier with the passage of time."

Dan nodded and his eyes met hers with an intense look of urgency. He gently took hold of her hands and let out a long sigh. "You really know how to bring it out of me, Detective. I don't know how to thank you for all you have already done for me, and for all you continue to do. You know how I feel. You've been there, too. All I can say is thanks."

Trace stared at him intently, not knowing what to say. She cherished his sincerity, his gentle warm touch, and everything about the moment. She prayed the moment would never end, yet something deep inside her knew it eventually had to.

CHAPTER 16
(Wednesday, March 2, – Thursday, March 3, 2016)

Silas drove through the small, quiet town of Pines, Pennsylvania around 10:30 p.m. He drove down the narrow streets past tall, stately brick and white shingled buildings that reminded him of castles. The brightly colored flower filled meadows surrounding the town were now only dark shadows silhouetted by the faint gleam of a half-moon shining above him. There were only a handful of people walking down the dimly-lit streets.

He hadn't been back home since he left in 2000 to join the Marines. Some buildings were familiar to him, while others seemed alien.

Earlier that evening, he had stopped at his favorite burger place for a greasy burger and fries, and now with his hunger for food satisfied, he would satisfy another more urgent need: revenge.

He approached the rutted dirt road lined with tall pine trees on either side, and headed toward his childhood home where his dad lived. At the end of the road, he pulled up into the blacktop driveway. Directly in front of him stood a moderate sized grey wooden house. He turned off the ignition and stared at the property for a few moments. Scanning the house's perimeter for his dad's old jeep, he realized the jeep was gone and so was his dad.

Silas remembered how scared he was when he was a boy and his dad would take him for hair-raising jeep races around the quarter acre property surrounding his house. He would hold on with all his might to the hand grip above the passenger door of the jeep, yet would always lose his grip and be thrown head first into the back seat. Silas recalled looking over at his dad, his face contorted in a hideous grin, as he whooped and hollered with wild abandon. Try as he might, he couldn't remember a time when his dad was not roaring drunk, sullen, and raging with anger toward him and his mother.

He knew his father, Jake Samuels, served in the Marines in the Vietnam war, was wounded in action, and received a medical discharge after three years of service. He returned from the war as a broken, changed man.

According to his mother, Martha, before entering the Marines Jake was a gentle and loving husband. He would always bring her roses for her birthday and special occasions, and would take her out for dinner. When his number came up in the draft in the mid-sixties, Martha begged him not to go, yet he was determined to serve his country as his dad did before him.

Silas recalled his mother telling him that when his dad

returned from Vietnam in the late sixties, he was in a lot of pain from severe shrapnel wounds to his legs and back. He underwent several surgeries to remove the shrapnel, which left him with a noticeable limp. He still had several pieces in his legs and back. Tired of seeing numerous doctors who told him there was nothing more they could do for him, he turned to alcohol and opiates to relieve his constant pain. Silas thought it was ironic that he also had a slight limp due to war-related leg wounds.

She even mentioned that she and Jake started arguing and fighting during her pregnancy with Silas. They attended a few couples therapy sessions, but his dad blamed her for his anger and violent tirades, and refused further therapy.

In his mind, Silas struggled to understand the man he called his dad. Try as he might, he couldn't fathom why his dad killed his loving mom and physically and sexually abused his own innocent son. He felt a rage welling up inside him the longer his dad kept him waiting. Reaching inside his camouflage jacket, he felt his Beretta inside the holster and this seemed to calm his rage momentarily.

Looking at his watch, he noticed it was now after midnight. He glanced at the old grey wooden house directly in front of his car, and studied it for a few moments. There was the same old wooden stairs leading to the front porch that was surrounded with a rickety decaying wood banister. The roof was vaulted with two large rectangular windows facing toward him, concealing the slanted shape attic room within. Silas recalled this was his bedroom and that he spent many hours staring out those same windows at nearby Pocono Lake.

He opened the car door and quietly slid out into the

pervasive darkness of the night. Turning up his collar against the chilly wind that met him, he walked toward the house and up the stairs to the front porch. He tried the doorknob to see if it was open, but discovered it was locked as he expected.

Smiling, he thought, *good thing you remembered to lock the door, dad. You never know who's lurking around the woods these days.*

Pulling the lock release gun from his coat pocket, he opened the door and walked in the house, locking the door behind him. He entered the living room area and scanned the room. A faint flicker of moonlight shone in through the heavy floor length drapes on the windows, silhouetting the couch that was to his left. Straight ahead of him was the staircase that led to the room in the attic that was once his bedroom. Silas had no intention of seeing the room that evoked too many painful memories. To his right was the fireplace, where his mom died all those years ago. The house had a heaviness in the air and a familiar musty odor.

On the coffee table in front of the couch, sat a bottle of vodka and a glass half full of the vile liquid that Silas despised as much as he despised his dad. An ashtray was full of cigarette butts and the butts spilled out of control onto the coffee table. A few remaining slices of pizza also lay on the table in a wide open delivery box.

Silas walked over to the couch and sat down. He picked up a slice of pizza, then threw it back down in the box. *I wonder how long the pizza has been lying on the table? Probably for the last thirty six years since he's lived here,* he mused.

Silas sat in the darkness with dark thoughts racing around his head, listening to the sound of his heartbeat pounding in his chest and in his ears. He also listened to the ambient noises in the house, the sounds of flies or other insects buzzing around him, and the hum of the refrigerator in the kitchen. Looking down at his watch, he pulled a flashlight out of his coat pocket and saw it read 12:20 a.m. *I wonder where he is? Probably in town at the local bar drinking himself into oblivion,* he surmised. *Drowning his sorrows with alcohol is what dad does best!*

Silas suddenly felt tired and realized he had been up for close to twelve hours, since the wee hours of the previous morning anticipating this meeting with Jake. He leaned his head back against the couch and soon fell into a deep slumber.

What started out as a dream about his mother when she was still alive, soon changed into another nightmare. His mother was standing outside the house in broad daylight and she was beckoning to him. There he was again as a little boy running toward her with the unbridled ecstasy of a child running through an open meadow. She held out her arms to him with a beaming smile on her face. He was just about to rush into her loving arms, when without warning she fell to the ground in a lifeless, crumbled heap.

He rushed over to her, but now she laid by the fireplace in some dream house in a pool of her own blood. As he gazed down at her, he noticed her eyes were wide open staring at him with an expression of absolute terror on her face that mirrored his own. "MOM!" he screamed as he knelt over her lifeless body. "PLEASE WAKE UP!" He felt so helpless and alone and tried to shake her, yet there was no response.

Intending to call 911 as his mother taught him, he ran into the dining room, but just as he lifted the receiver his dad knocked the phone from his hand and laughed that wicked, hideous laugh of his… Silas shook with terror at the thought of being alone with his dad…

A loud noise woke him from his nightmare. It was the sound of screeching brakes of a vehicle pulling up to the house. He sat bolt upright on the couch, covered with a chilling sweat, as was his usual nightmare routine. He wryly smiled at the thought of his dad's shocked expression when he saw his long lost son sitting right in front of his eyes. *Things were different now, and his dad would have to face the vengeance of his hateful adult son!* Breathing heavily, he listened and heard the sound of the front door lock being opened. In the dimly lit room, Silas watched his dad enter the front room and stagger drunkenly toward the stairway.

The room now reeked with the smell of alcohol. His back was facing Silas as he removed his dark grey wool coat and tan baseball cap and draped them over the bannister. Silas' immediate instinct was to pounce on him, yet he held back and continued watching his dad and waiting for just the right moment to make his presence known.

Jake turned and stumbled his way past the couch where Silas sat. He headed toward the kitchen and mumbled something about getting "some grub…" He turned on a light in the kitchen and started feverishly looking for something he was unable to find. After five minutes of his futile searching, he staggered his way back to the front room and noticed the pizza box sitting open on the coffee table. He grabbed for a piece of pizza and hungrily stuffed the entire piece in his mouth.

Silas watched him with a hatred that seethed deep inside him, ready to erupt like lava spewing forth from a volcano. He decided this was the moment he had anticipated, for so many agonizing years.

"Had enough to eat and drink, Dad?" he asked in a mocking tone of voice.

Jake stood in a dead silence glaring at the sinister figure sitting on his couch. Recognizing his son, he stopped chewing and swallowed hard. Finally finding his voice after a few moments, he cleared his throat and rasped at Silas. "What in hell brings you here?"

Silas grinned and with a restrained composure replied, "Why of course, you damn well know the reason. Just in case you don't, I think it's high time that father and son have a little chat." His and dad's eyes locked.

Jake's face now flushed with anger. "Not now at 1 o'clock in the morning, goddamn it!" he bellowed.

Silas continued to smile nonchalantly at his dad. "I say there's no time like the present, Dad. We have a lot of time to make up for, don't we? Let's see now…" he paused for effect. "As a matter of fact, we have thirty six years to catch up on."

"There's nothing to catch up on. Nothing much has changed," Jake waved his hand in mid-air to emphasize his point.

"You know what I see? I see a very angry, lonely, bitter man. You were angry at Mom and me all the time! In fact, everything we did made you angry, Dad. I was just a kid and bore the brunt of your anger. So, I'd like to know what I did that made you so angry?"

Jake and Silas locked eyes again. Jake looked as though the volcano was ready to explode in him as well.

"You took after your mother," he spat out his words at

Silas. "She spent more time mothering you than being a wife to me! We used to spend lots of time together before you came along." He stared down at the floor.

"Ok, so now you're blaming me for being born? I don't think I had anything to do with the conception, Dad. Every time I watched the two of you together, you were fighting and arguing. I think the whole crux of the matter was that she didn't like the lunatic her drunken husband had become!" Silas glared at his dad and reached in his coat pocket and fingered the holster and Beretta.

Jake was still staring down at the floor and now held his head with his hands.

"I served my time for my country, like you, and where did it get me?" he yelled at Silas. "It left me crippled and with constant horrid memories. You think that's easy to deal with?" Jake leaned toward Silas with his face flushed with anger and veins bulging on his forehead.

"You didn't have to take it out on me and Mom, Dad! You could've got counseling, like Mom did. Instead, you chose to drown your sorrows in alcohol and opiates. You inflicted your vile fury on Mom and me, the two people who least deserved it!"

Silas shifted his weight on the couch and savored the fact that he had made his point. Jake was silent for a few moments. He walked across the room toward a small lamp next to a dirty faded brown armchair with springs sticking up out of its overused seat cushion. He turned on the small lamp and wearily sank down into the chair. Silas studied every detail of his dad as if to retain every last memory for posterity. This moment was finally his revenge and reward. He noticed his dad's weary, pensive facial expression, his disheveled and thinning grey hair, grease smeared dark green t-shirt, and worn baggy blue jeans. *He's lost a lot of weight,* Silas thought. *Probably from all the drinking and smoking…*

Studying the look of resignation on his face, Silas momentarily felt something that tugged at his heart and caused him great conflict. Here was his dad, an old, broken, angry alcoholic with nothing to show for his life except leaving a legacy as a murderer and abuser. *Is that the legacy I want to leave?* He realized that his dad's legacy of murder and abuse was also his own, and not by choice. He felt the anger once again rising within him.

His dad's raspy voice interrupted his thoughts. "If you're here to chew me out for being such a bastard, don't waste your time," he growled. Baring his teeth, Silas pulled out his Beretta and fired a shot at his dad's knee. Jake howled in pain and grabbed his knee. He fell off his chair and writhed in agony on the blood-stained carpet.

"Well, now that we're on that topic, glad you brought that up!" Silas shot back at him. I have a question for you, you son of a bitch! Why in hell did you have to kill her?" Silas stood clenching his jaw and fists.

"She deserved it!" Jake yelled up at him from the floor with spittle flying from his mouth.

"You son of a bitch! She did nothing to deserve a bastard like you for a husband! What about your son? Did he also deserve to be abused by his son of a bitch father?"

Calmer now, Silas walked over toward him and smugly studied his pathetic features for a few moments.

"So, Dad, how does it feel to be on the receiving end?"

He sardonically grinned, enjoying his dad's agony.

Jake groveled on the floor, still clutching his knee, and yelled up at Silas. "You're my son, I'm sorry to admit, and therefore, you're just as pathetic as I am!"

"Perhaps, Dad, but just remember that it was you who created the monster. That's the legacy you chose to leave! You could have had a loving son and wife, yet you didn't deserve us!"

Jake momentarily stopped writhing and father and son locked eyes. "Go ahead and do what you need to do! Kill me!"

Silas waited a bit longer to savor the moment and take in every detail of his dad begging for his suffering to end. Silas also wanted an end to his own suffering. "This is for Mom and me!" Resolutely lifting his Beretta, he fired a shot right between his dad's eyes.

Silas looked at his dad's lifeless body and saw his head was bent back at a grotesque angle with mouth agape and wide eyes staring sightlessly up at the ceiling. He smiled, and for the first time in thirty six years, he felt a heavy weight lifted from his shoulders. He carefully placed his Beretta back in its holster and walked toward the door.

Exiting the house, he walked around to the garage next to the house and retrieved a can of gasoline that his dad stored there. He took the can of gasoline and after dousing the house, he pulled a small matchbook out of his pocket, lit the whole matchbook and threw it toward the house.

From a safe distance, he watched the house burning, and felt an immense sense of relief and joy he hadn't experienced in a long time. He got into his car and raced away, leaving agonizing childhood memories behind in a blaze of flames and glory.

CHAPTER 17
(Thursday, March 3, 2016)

Trace awoke to the sound of her cell chimes that disturbed her slumber. Reaching for her cell, she noticed the white digital reading of 6:45 a.m. shining back at her. Listening to the message, she smiled at Dan's voicemail letting her know he made it back to Archer last night around midnight.

She sleepily yawned and lingered in bed for a few extra minutes, recalling the events of the past few days. She smiled when remembering Dan holding her hands at Dino's during lunch a few days prior, and the sincerity in his voice. Her heart skipped a beat when she recalled the tenderness in his eyes. *Okay, Detective, this is professional, remember,* she chided herself.

After their sharing of more relationship memories for a good part of their long eight hour drive home the previous day, Trace felt a definite connection to Dan. She probably felt a bit more than she wanted to feel. Dan insisted that he drop her off at home late last night rather than her office, only two blocks away from home. She was glad she didn't have to walk home alone.

When she got home, she received a call from Jennie, tearfully informing her that Sean had passed away. Trace spent at least an hour on the phone trying to comfort her. She made a mental note to try to reconnect with her when she got home from her busy day.

The sound of her cell chiming again brought her back to the present. It was Officer Murray from WPD returning the message she left the previous night after Dan dropped her off.

Trace glanced at the clock on her nightstand and noticed it was 7:15 a.m. After listening to his message confirming their 9 a.m. meeting, she hurriedly got out of bed, dressed and made it to WPD a few minutes late.

Walking in the front door, she was greeted by the receptionist, a jolly middle-aged lady named Jodi. "Hey Malone. How's it going? Officers Murray and Ramsey are waiting for you in your office," she cheerily smiled as Trace rushed by her desk.

"Thanks so much, Jodi." Trace entered her office and closed the door behind her. In front of her stood Officers Murray and Ramsey, and they all greeted each other. She enjoyed the camaraderie they all shared from working together on several previous cases. She sat behind her desk and let out a long sigh. "I'm sorry for being late. I had a late night last night after a long drive to Maine to visit a client."

Murray and Ramsey sat back down in their chairs and Murray was the first to speak. "That's okay, Detective. No worries. I was glad when you called me because we have some information for you about our murder suspect and his last victim. First and foremost, I'd like to say how much we admired your dad and miss seeing him around the station when he did his volunteer work rehabilitating prisoners. He was such a kind, honorable man."

Trace blushed and held back tears as she thought about her dad and how much she missed him. "Thanks, Murray. I miss him too. He taught me a lot…" her voice trailed off. Pausing to regain her composure, she reached on the floor under her desk for her black tote bag and pulled out her notepad and pen. "I have some information to share about the client I just visited who's also involved in this case. You can go first, guys."

Murray nodded and began his report. "I'm sure you heard about our perp's latest victim, Jackie Hugo. Trace nodded. "Yes, I've been in her store a few times. How is she doing by the way?"

"She was treated for a broken nose and minor facial lacerations and released from the hospital. She gave me a fairly good description of the guy, and I got a good look at him as well. My partner here also found his black trench coat hanging on a hanger in the clothing section of Ms. Hugo's store."

Trace looked puzzled. "That's strange that he would leave his coat as evidence to be used against him, unless he wanted to change his wardrobe. Were there any fingerprints found on the coat?"

"It's still being inspected at present. Ramsey found something interesting; some old bullet casings in one of the pockets."

Ramsey shifted his seated position and placed one foot

on his other knee. Clearing his throat, he announced, "The casings appear to be from a semiautomatic pistol, possibly a Beretta. We can compare the casings to other casings, if any, found at the various crime scenes where Samuels was."

Trace pulled a long strand of untethered blonde hair behind her ear and leaned in toward the officers. "Until recently, Samuels has used a knife as his main weapon. I had an encounter with him last week and he fired his gun at me. He quickly escaped out the window, so I didn't get a good look at the gun. These casings are a good lead for us."

Ramsey nodded. "According to Ms. Hugo, our perp pointed a gun at her head. She was lucky that we arrived when we did or she might not have survived."

Trace paused for a moment remembering what Ramsey said about Silas' gun. "Have these casings already been confirmed?"

Ramsey planted both feet on the floor and leaned forward toward Trace. "You're gonna find this interesting, Detective. After we left Hugo's store, we paid a visit to a few of the neighborhood businesses, including a rather unsavory business, Jose's Garage, aka: Jose's Car Painting. We've had our eyes on this business for a while and have observed a lot of traffic in and out of the place, specifically, during late night and early morning hours. We had a chat with Tony, the owner, and after informing him of his rights, he gave us a lot of insight on Samuels. It appears that Samuels had his Camaro repainted. Tony also told us that Samuels held a gun to his head and he saw it was a Beretta." Ramsey leaned back into his chair and smugly folded his arms.

Trace thoughtfully scribbled a few notes in her notepad,

then glanced up at Ramsey. "What color is his car now?"

"Silver with new plates and registration, and new ID. Samuels is now Stuart Wyatt. We can get you the car information when we're finished."

Trace nodded and glanced at the officers with an amused expression on her face. "He's indeed a man of many talents. Did Silas, or Stuart, tell Tony where he was headed in his repainted car?"

Murray added his input. "Tony said he had the car waiting for our perp and saw him speed off toward Highway 7 South. Where he went from there, we're not sure. It could be anywhere from Connecticut to New York, or even Massachusetts. We have an APB on him."

Trace nodded and smiled. "Good work, guys."

"Thanks, Detective. What further information do you have for us?" Murray inquired.

"So, you guys are probably familiar with Silas' other victims, George and Susan Adams up in Lakeland, Maine, Dan Stevens from Archer, and Jennie Andrews and her boyfriend, Sean Johnson?" Murray and Ramsey both nodded. "Dan Stevens is my client, and as you probably already know, his wife and youngest daughter were killed, and his oldest daughter, Annie, is still recuperating in the hospital. I recently visited with Jennie and Sean. Jennie is pretty traumatized by her attack and the loss of Sean who recently passed away from severe injuries to his chest and heart."

Murray shifted in his chair. "Sorry to hear about Sean, and your client's wife and daughter. What injuries did Jennie sustain?"

"She had a rape test done and she's following up with

her doctor. She also has a wrist fracture, black eye, and facial bruising. This was when Silas and I had a bit of a wrestling match, as I previously mentioned."

Trace felt a shudder of revulsion run through her as she recalled her first encounter with Silas aka: Stuart. Murray's question brought her back to the present.

"What's the status of George and Susan Adams?"

"Dan and I visited them yesterday and they are still in the hospital recovering from their surgeries. Susan was pregnant and was stabbed in her belly, initiating early delivery of her baby, Lynette, who is in NICU on life support. It's a pretty sad situation. They don't know if the baby is gonna survive."

The officers and detective were all silent for a few moments. A knock on the door interrupted their interlude.

Ramsey got up and walked over to see who was at the door. It was Jodi the receptionist with an urgent message for the officers. Just as Trace reached for her tote bag and prepared to leave, Ramsey hurried back into the room holding a piece of paper Jodi had handed him. He conferred with Murray for a few minutes, then they both approached Trace.

"Detective, don't leave so fast," Ramsey warned. "Jodi informed me that the Police Department in Pines, PA just called to inform us about a fire situation that could involve our perp."

Trace stared pensively at Ramsey and Murray and let out a long sigh. *Well, the catnap and chat with Jennie would have to wait,* she thought. "Just like old times, right guys? Guess we're taking a road trip."

CHAPTER 18
(Thursday March 3, 2016)

Dan sat in his Mustang in the driveway, thoughtfully gazing at the house he used to live in during happier times. *Had it really been two weeks since that fateful day when everything in my life instantly changed,* he wondered.

He remembered times in the recent past when his family was all together sitting in the front room watching TV. Tears welled up in his eyes as he recalled times spent with his daughters at the school playground and at the beach. Echoes of their laughter simultaneously filled his ears and heart with joy and overwhelming sadness.

His eyes followed the stately lines of his house and the steep, dark grey roofline upwards to the multi-paned bedroom windows. He focused his attention on the bedroom he once shared with Peggy. Memories of their intense love-making suddenly overcame him. Holding his head in his hands, he allowed himself to shed the bitter tears of anger and sadness flooding his eyes. *Peggy, my love, I miss you so much and wish you were here with me back in my arms again.*

Instantly, his mind wandered to the previous night when he drove Trace back to her house. The way she looked at him as they stood for a few moments in her driveway before they said goodnight. Everything about her was attractive to him, and he longed to embrace her and… no, he shook his head as if that would rid his mind of those thoughts. *It's too soon… or is it?*

Dan was startled from his reverie by the sound of his cell phone ringing. It was Dr. Wilson calling to give him a report on Annie.

"Hi, Dr. Wilson. How's Annie doing?"

"Well, Dan, I have some good and bad news. So, here's the bad news. Annie has developed bacterial pneumonia and she's now receiving IV antibiotics and nebulizer treatments. She's pretty sleepy, as is common with pneumonia, and she needs at least another few weeks in the hospital. I know you are looking forward to taking her home."

Dan paused for a few minutes as he listened to Dr. Wilson. "So, what's the good news?"

"We transferred her from ICU to a regular floor today. She's also asking for you."

"I'm leaving now."

Dan disconnected the call and drove to the hospital in record time. He parked his car in the outside lot and ran into the hospital. After asking the front desk clerk for Annie's room number, he took the elevator to the sixth floor.

He passed the nurse's desk and a nurse asked him who he was visiting. The nurse told him to put on a mask and gloves before entering Annie's room. After donning mask and gloves, he entered and found her lying on her side in bed facing the door. She still had an IV in her right hand and was receiving a nebulizer treatment from a respiratory therapist standing next to her bed. Annie recognized him as he approached her bed, and instantly sat up and pulled the nebulizer tube out of her mouth. "Daddy, Daddy!" she smiled and tried to sit up.

"Hi, sweetheart. You need to lie back and rest." He walked over to the other side of her bed across from the therapist and gently held her shoulders to keep her from getting out of bed. He apologetically looked at the woman therapist. She smiled and informed him that the treatment was finished.

The therapist placed Annie's regular oxygen mask on her face and left the room. Annie looked at him and started to cry. "Daddy, I missed you. Where did you go?" She had a long coughing fit. Dan smoothed her long auburn tresses with his gloved hand, trying to comfort her.

"Honey, I went up to Maine for a few days to visit my friend, George from the Marines. He is also in the hospital."

She wiped her eyes with her free hand, and gazed at him with wide brown eyes. "Daddy, is he sick?"

Dan shook his head and smiled at her. "No, sweetheart. He was injured in an accident like you were."

"What happened to him?"

Dan paused for a few moments trying to find the right words to explain a murderer and his motives to a child. He thought it was best to not add more stress to her current situation.

"He was in a fight."

"Oh, okay." Annie thoughtfully paused for a few seconds.

"Like I was, daddy?"

Dan stared intently at her. "What do you mean?"

Annie's voice was just a whisper that was muffled by her oxygen mask. "I had a dream last night about a man who was trying to hurt me. You were in the dream and so was Mom and Steph."

Dan tenderly touched her cheek. "Sweetheart, that was just a dream," he tried to reassure her. "Nobody's going to hurt you. I promise. You're safe here in the hospital."

Dan noticed Annie was having a hard time staying awake and saw her eyes fluttering.

"Are Mom and Steph here, too?"

"Mom and Steph are safe as well."

"Will I get better, Daddy?"

"Yes, Annie, you have a lung infection called pneumonia. That's why you have that oxygen mask on your face to help you breathe." Dan noticed her eyes were now closed. He reached for her hand and held it for a few moments.

"Get some sleep now, Annie. I love you."

"Love you too…" Annie muttered and soon fell into a deep slumber.

Dan stayed with Annie a few extra minutes and then left her room. He threw his mask and gloves into the garbage bin outside her room and walked over to the nurses' station. He asked one of the nurses sitting at the desk if Dr. Wilson was available. The nurse nodded and Dan heard Dr. Wilson's page over the intercom system. He walked over to the lounge and read a magazine while he waited.

Shortly thereafter, Dr. Wilson appeared and they exchanged greetings. Dan informed him of his conversation with

Annie and inquired, "Has she ever mentioned to you that she had a dream about a man trying to harm her?"

Dr. Wilson solemnly nodded. "Yes, she's told me about quite a few dreams she's been having recently all related to that topic. I think it best to keep it low key right now. Her body needs to recover from the pneumonia. She may eventually need to talk with a therapist about the traumatic situation she endured. She'll hopefully be better able to deal with her situation when she's stronger."

Dan stared down at the floor. "I told her it was only a dream, and I wish it was."

CHAPTER 19
(Thursday, March 3, 2016)

Trace stared out the window at the beautiful shoreline of Lake Champlain as they drove from Waterton south along Highway 87 toward Pines, Pennsylvania. Murray was driving and talking with Ramsey who sat next to him in the front passenger seat. Trace sat in the back seat adding to the conversation when she felt like she had something to say.

She was preoccupied with thoughts about Silas' history and wondered what she would find out about him and his family. She also pondered a question that plagued her from the moment the sheriff had contacted her to help with this case. *How did Silas get contact information on his squad mates?* She meant to ask the sheriff when they were back in Archer, but there were always other mysteries to ponder.

The ring of Trace's cell roused her out of her preoccupation. She looked at the number and didn't recognize it, yet the call was from Lakeland, Maine, so she answered it.

"Hello, Detective Malone. This is Detective Mike Randolph, the guy who bumped into you, or rather your client, Dan, when you visited George and Susan. I've been wanting to connect with you to share some important findings. Is this a good time for us to chat?"

"Yes, Detective. This is as good a time as any. What are your findings?"

"Well, I have some news about Samuels."

"It's interesting you should happen to call. I was just thinking about him as well."

"Then great minds think alike, as the saying goes. Anyway, I think you'll find this interesting. I have been doing some investigating on my end and came upon this information quite by accident. When George and I first met, I asked him for any details about his assailant that he could recall and that's when he remembered the dog tags Samuels wore around his neck. After further investigation, I found out about Samuels' court-martial and ensuing prison time and discharge. I thought it was strange that he still wore them fifteen years after leaving the service."

Trace listened with interest as Randolph spoke. "So, what do you think is the connection?"

"Dog tags contain very private information, especially name, rank and social security number and as you know, identity theft is huge nowadays. It would be very easy for this information to be hacked if it fell into the wrong hands."

"Yes, agreed. I'm starting to see a correlation here that Silas possibly had some access to his squad mates' private information prior to his court-martial. How do you think he accomplished this?"

"Detective, you are on the right track. He could have taken down some names and phone numbers when they first started their training. But it actually goes deeper than that.

When I was working on another case that involved identity theft, I discovered a covert hacking operation disguised as a business. When contacting this business, I talked with several people before I talked to the right person who informed me how this business operates, and therein lies the connection to Silas. I found out that Silas used to work for this organization, and apparently he did his job well. He had a great rapport with his boss. In fact, he could very well have been paid some good money and could have easily risen through the ranks to supervisor or even higher."

"Had he not left to pay his mates a visit and exact his revenge," Trace interjected. "He gains the favor of his boss by doing everything that's expected of him, then does his own hacking of the Military Records to locate his victims."

Randolph smiled. "That's correct, Detective. My theory about Silas wearing his tags for all these years is that he was either trying to keep his own identity safe, or a secret."

Trace pondered the information that Randolph delivered. "Have you placed an APB to other stations about this information you've told me? Do you have any idea where this organization is located?

"As related to your first question, I just learned about this today actually, and conveyed this information to Lakeland Police Headquarters. They are working on the APB as we speak. In regards to your second question, not yet. Although, I have a hunch it might be someplace familiar to Silas."

"I'm heading up to Pines, PA, with my officer buddies, Murray and Ramsey, to investigate a fire situation that involves Silas. I will definitely convey the information you shared with me to the Pines Police Department and see what information they already have on Silas."

"Do you have any further information for me?" Randolph asked.

"At this point, we know very little other than this fire situation. I will keep you posted when I learn more. Thanks so much for sharing this information with me. This puts together another piece of the puzzle."

"Glad to help, Detective. Keep in touch and be safe."

Trace disconnected the call and shared her news with Murray and Ramsey.

After a long six hour drive, they arrived at the Pines Police Department. They walked into the ranch style brown trim building and approached the front desk. Trace introduced herself and the officers to the solemn-faced woman secretary wearing her name badge, Sgt. Jeri Jacobs, pinned to her uniform. Jeri told them to have a seat, and within a few minutes they were greeted by Officer Fred Tomlinson. After they exchanged introductions, the officer escorted them down a long hall to his office.

Entering the office, Trace noticed another female officer wearing glasses and her jet black hair in a tight bun, sitting behind a large mahogany desk. They all took their seats, and Officer Tomlinson was the first to speak. Waving his hand at the woman officer, Tomlinson declared, "This is Officer Sheila Berryman, who is also a crime scene investigator. She'll be helping us with this case." Trace was the first to get up to shake her hand, with Murray and Ramsey following close behind. Sheila greeted them all with a smile as she began her narrative.

"Officers and Detective Malone, thanks so much for traveling all the way from Waterton to Pines today. We appreciate your prompt arrival and attention to this case. We have a lot of information and evidence to share with you today." Turning her chair toward Trace, she continued her report. "Detective Malone, I know you are currently working with your client and former Marine, Dan Stevens, who along with his wife and daughters were victims of heinous crimes committed by our ruthless murderer." She then addressed Murray and Ramsey. "Officers, we also know you were on the scene in Waterton with another victim, Jackie Hugo, who is the owner of a local curio shop. Well, we found definitive evidence in a house in our area that was set ablaze by our suspect."

The detective and officers stared attentively at Sheila. "So, here's what we know about the house that was recently set on fire. After our interrogation of a neighbor, we found out this house belonged to one Jake Samuels, who is actually Silas' or Stuart's father. His neighbor reported the fire and the fire department got there in time to salvage a bunch of evidence, such as shell casings from Silas' Beretta, and the charred remains of his father's body."

Ramsey spoke next. "I also found a few shell casings from his gun in the pocket of his black trench coat left at the store of Jackie Hugo after he attacked her. My guess is that he left the coat and did a quick wardrobe change because he knew the coat made him more visible."

Sheila looked thoughtful. "Hopefully, the shell casings

you found will be the same as the ones we found."

Ramsey nodded his agreement. "That's the best case scenario. If not, then other evidence will confirm that Silas is our guy. Do you know what compelled him to kill his own father?"

"We are still investigating that very topic, Officer Ramsey. During our interview with Mr. Samuels's neighbor, Richard Gray, he told us that he often heard heated arguments between Samuels and his wife, Martha. We also found several police reports of suspected domestic abuse. Mr. Gray also reported that Mrs. Samuels died an untimely death at an early age. The forensic reports stated that Mrs. Samuels died from a traumatic brain hemorrhage, yet how the injury occurred is still inconclusive. The case went to court on allegations made by the defense lawyer that Samuels pushed his wife into the brick fireplace, causing her fatal brain hemorrhage. Samuels denied his guilt, stating that his wife tripped and fell, hitting her head on the fireplace wall. Samuels was found innocent based on insubstantial evidence."

Trace thoughtfully scribbled down notes in her notepad. "How convenient," she mused. "Are you aware of the other victims involved in this case?"

"Yes, we also know about the attacks on George and Susan Adams and their baby, and that other members of the squadron, Griffin and Nielson, are also in danger. These are the victims and potential ones we are currently aware of. Are there more, Detective?"

Trace nodded and informed her about Jennie Andrews and Sean Johnson, and her encounter with Silas. She also informed the CSI and officers about Jennie's fragile health status and Sean's death. Tomlinson exchanged glances with Sheila, and remarked, "Thanks for bringing us up to date on these victims and their statuses, Detective. Is there anything else you need to report?"

"Yes, as a matter of fact. You previously mentioned that my client's squadron mates, Sergeant Joe Griffin and Master Sergeant Nielson are the logical next targets for our suspect. I would suggest our next APB be sent immediately to Adirondacks PD where Griffin resides and to Brightport Police Headquarters, where Nielson resides. I spoke to a detective on the drive up here about Silas' source for locating his victims, and he was a plethora of information. It seems there's an underground hacking organization that Silas used to work for and that's how he gathered this information. We're still trying to figure out where this company is located."

Tomlinson glanced at Trace and nodded. "Thanks, Detective. I will see to it that Sgt. Jacobs gets right on this. In the meantime, my partner here will fill you in on our findings in this case." Tomlinson stood up from his chair and left the office.

Murray was the next to speak. "I'm sure you also know from our last APB that Samuels, our suspect, has had his car and ID changed. He is now driving a silver Camaro, and he goes by the name of Stuart Wyatt."

At that moment, Officer Tomlinson entered the office. After announcing that Jacobs notified special surveillance units at Adirondacks and Brightport Police Departments, he took his seat next to his partner. Sheila updated him on their conversation.

Leaning his elbow into the armrest on his swivel chair, he announced, "Ok, so if Samuels' mother died at an early age,

Samuels was also pretty young when she was killed by his father. This sounds like as good a reason as any to even the score
with his dad."

Trace busily scribbled down some notes on her notepad and glanced at the officers. "Can I get a copy of the police
forensics report?"

Sheila smiled and handed her a manila envelope. "I
made you a few copies." Looking at her watch, she noticed it
was 5 p.m. "Anything else you'd like to ask before we ad-
journ?" Murray leaned forward toward Sheila. "What other
evidence was found at the house?"

"Tomorrow morning we'll drive over there. If it's more
evidence you're looking for, I think you all will have a field
day."

After they thanked the officers, Trace walked out with
Murray and Ramsey to their squad car. When they reached the
car, she turned to face them. "So, guys, your place or mine?"
They all laughed to break the tension of the day and headed
into town to get some dinner and find a motel for the night.

CHAPTER 20
(Friday, March 4, 2016) 8:10 a.m.

Joe Griffin left his red, rustic two-level log cabin early in the morning to hike around beautiful Lang Lake near his property outside of Adirondack, New York.

After his three mile hike, he paused for a rest outside his cabin and surveyed the heavily wooded fourteen acres surrounding his cabin. Beads of sweat from the hike dripped down his chocolate brown-skinned cheek as he breathed in the chilly mountain air. He enjoyed the solitude and sweeping vistas of the Adirondack Mountains from where he stood.

Gazing up at the sky, he took in the amazing peach, magenta, and lavender rays of the eastern sunrise that radiated the beginnings of a new day.

Slowly sauntering toward the front door of his cabin, he recalled memories of when he first moved to this area fifteen years prior, after leaving the Marines. He had the good fortune of buying the cabin from a good friend at a good price. He smiled as he recalled memories of him and his dad, a skilled electrician, working together on bringing the electrical wiring throughout the cabin up to code. A stipend from his time served in the Marines enabled Joe to obtain certification as an electrician. This place afforded him the luxury of working from home and provided respite from painful combat memories.

As he walked toward the cabin entrance, he thought he heard the sound of an approaching vehicle. *I'm not expecting any visitors,* he thought. Suddenly remembering his neighbor often used his tractor to plow his land, he breathed a sigh of relief.

He entered the cabin and walked through the kitchen to the front room and down the long hallway to the bathroom. His landline phone rang several times, but he wasn't expecting any calls from anyone. He listened to the familiar answering machine greeting. "Hey, this is Joe. I'm not here right now, so please leave your message." He then heard the voice message of a woman who introduced herself as an officer from the Adirondacks Police Department. He couldn't hear the rest of the message. Joe pulled his cell out of his hiking pants pocket intending to call the APD and noticed the battery was dead.

After finishing his business in the bathroom, he hurried down the hallway toward the front room where his landline phone was perched on a coffee table next to the sofa.

From out of nowhere, a man wearing a black face mask and camouflage jacket lunged at him and knocked him to the floor. Instinctively, his martial arts training kicked in and he swung his elbow hard into his attacker's face and heard a crunching sound. The man suddenly released his strangle grip around Joe's throat, and Joe delivered another punch to the man's face. Momentarily stunned, the man lie motionless on the floor.

Seeing his chance, Joe turned to run into the kitchen for his gun, when the man swiftly reached up and grabbed Joe's foot. He landed heavily on the floor on his belly and the man flung his body on top of him. The man tried to pin Joe's arms behind his back, but Joe was able to wrestle his arms free. He grabbed for the man's head and pulled off his mask instead. He thrust his head upward and forcefully butted his head back toward his attacker's face. The man yelped in pain and rolled off Joe onto his side. Seeing his advantage, Joe rolled onto his back and leaped into an upright position. He glared down at the man's profusely bleeding face and instantly recognized his attacker. "Silas, you son of a bitch!" Grabbing Silas' arm, he twisted it behind his back and kneeled with all his weight down on his shoulder.

"So, Joe, we meet again." Silas gritted his teeth at the pain Joe inflicted on him. He tried to kick his leg up toward Joe's face, but a fierce karate chop to his carotid knocked him out cold.

The sound of the phone ringing brought Silas back to consciousness. He was now lying on his back on the floor. He opened his eyes to see Joe standing above him pointing his Glock 19 at Silas' chest.

Joe glared down at Silas with a scowl on his face. "Give me one good reason I shouldn't blast you straight into hell, coward!" Before Silas could speak, a voice message was heard coming from Joe's answering machine. "This is Sergeant Jacobs from the Pines Police Department. I've been trying to reach you, Mr. Griffin, to inform you that we have alerted the Adirondacks Police Department special surveillance unit about your situation. They will be contacting you soon, if they haven't already."

The sound of sirens blaring in the distance distracted Joe's attention, and he momentarily turned his head to take a quick glance out his window. Silas' voice interrupted him. "Maybe you should get back to them, Joe, and tell them their services won't be needed."

In a flash, Silas leapt up and lunged at Joe, knocking him back down onto the floor. Joe fired a shot at Silas, grazing his shoulder as he landed on top of Joe. Silas again gritted his teeth and kneed Joe in the groin. Joe doubled over in pain, and the next head punch from Silas turned his world to black.

Joe wasn't sure how long he was unconscious, yet he sensed his body being dragged along the floor. After several moments, he groggily regained consciousness and once again heard sirens, this time closer to the house.

Quickly opening his eyes, he found himself sitting upright in a chair in the front room with duct tape tightly wrapped around his mouth, hands and feet. His hands were tied behind his back and his feet were bound together with duct tape. His head and face ached, one eye was swollen shut, and blood streamed from his nostrils. The taste of blood in his mouth made him want to vomit.

Silas stood directly in front of him holding his Beretta to Joe's head. Joe struggled to free his hands from his bonds, but they held fast. Silas had a hideous grin on his blood-streaked face, and he held his free hand over his lanced shoulder.

"So here's the deal, Joe. Ever since the court-martial,

my life has been a living hell. I've had to scrounge around for work, my pay is minimal, I can't get any insurance, and I've had to live in my car. That's what I get for serving my country! But, you wouldn't know anything about that, would you, Joe?"

The phone rang again, and this time the officer announced that his surveillance unit had arrived at Joe's place. He tried to turn his head around to face the window, yet the slightest movement caused an intense explosion of facial pain. He noticed the window shades were closed to darken the room.

The two surveillance officers standing outside the two story log cabin approached the front entrance with their guns held directly in front of them. Pointing to a silver Camaro partially hidden in a nearby grove of pine trees, one officer signaled to his partner who headed toward the car.

"So, Joe, this time it's your turn to give me a good reason I shouldn't blast YOU straight into hell," Silas sneered. "Should I let them know you're tied up at the moment?" Joe glared at Silas with his one good eye and met his sinister gaze and mocking smile. Joe tried to lean forward in his chair as close to Silas' face as he could get as if daring him to finish the job. *My last hope is that the police riddle your ass so full of bullet holes that you die a more horrible death than I will,* he cursed under his breath.

Hearing voices outside, Silas walked over to the window and peeked out from behind the closed shade. He observed an officer approaching and pondered his escape route. Pacing around the house, he scanned the upstairs loft area and noticed a short wooden staircase that he presumed led out to the roof. Smiling with relief, he then raced back to the front room where Joe was sitting. Silas' last words echoed in Joe's brain. "Okay, asshole. Sorry to shoot and run, yet it looks like your time is up. Thanks for ratting on me in court. One more to go and the playing field is leveled!" Joe's last vision was of Silas' face contorted with hatred pointing his Beretta at Joe's head.

A shot was fired and Joe slumped forward. There was a crashing sound of splintering wood.

Racing upstairs, Silas climbed the rickety wooden ladder leading up to the attic. Glancing back toward the kitchen, he saw the officer break through the front door and run toward Joe.

He pressed his good shoulder into the small hatch door above him and shoved his hand into the handle. It opened with a cracking noise, and Silas slid his body into the attic. Slowly making his way through the dark and gloomy attic, he found the exit door and crawled outside onto the roof.

He ran toward the edge of the roof, and noticed an enclosed porch beneath the roof. Sliding down the roof, he ran toward the bannister surrounding the porch and jumped over the railing. Finding himself suddenly airborne, he landed on the ground ten feet below, cat style on all fours.

Running toward his Camaro, he heard another shot fired behind him that ricocheted off a nearby tree. Turning around as he ran, he saw an officer running toward him with his gun held in front of him. Silas fired a few shots from his gun, and saw the officer fall to the ground clutching his leg.

Breathlessly sprinting the last fifty feet toward his car, he finally reached it. He flung open the door and turned the ignition key. The motor sputtered a few times, then went silent. Silas pounded his hand on the steering wheel and winced in pain. "C'mon, baby, don't fail me now!" he yelled.

After a few more trics, the engine purred to life. Silas raced down the dirt road, his tires hurdling rocks and gravel like projectile missiles at the squad car pursuing him. Silas glanced in his rearview mirror at the advancing squad car. He put his foot on the accelerator and felt his Camaro swerving from side to side on thc rutted, desolate dirt road leaving Griffin's property. Cursing to himself, he wished he could have been driving in his dad's old Jeep. *That car really got around,* he thought.

The sound of a police siren and flashing lights in his side mirror brought him back to the present. His Camaro swerved and skidded about fifty feet farther down the road and Silas noticed a fine mix of snow and rain started to coat the windshield. He eventually pulled the car over to the side. The squad car also pulled over. Both drivers sat in their vehicles waiting for the other to make a move.

Silas nervously drummed his fingers on the steering wheel and kept his eye on his rearview mirror. The squad car's red and blue flashers danced wildly around his car and lit up the pristine, cold white winter landscape. Silas watched the now swirling white snowflakes that silently fell all around him. They were strangely comforting.

I know this cop is checking the plates and he needs to go and so do I, he reminded himself. Reaching inside his jacket, he found his holster and pulled out his Beretta. He pushed the mag release button, released the old magazine, and reloaded a new one. With one hand resting on the door handle, he waited for the officer.

The officer slowly opened the door of his squad car and cautiously approached Silas' car. Silas watched him through the side mirror and holding his breath, he waited for the right moment to make his move.

When the officer was halfway to his Camaro, Silas lunged out the door, landing with a thud on the ground with his Beretta held in readiness. Taking aim, he fired several shots at the officer, hitting him in the chest and neck. The officer fell to the ground, firing his own gun toward Silas as he fell. One bullet ricocheted off his front driver side tire, and the other grazed Silas' leg.

Wincing in pain, he hobbled his way back to the Camaro and after checking the tire, took off down the road. Glancing back in his rearview mirror, he noticed the officer was lying motionless in the middle of the road. His mouth curled into a sly smile as he thought, *I guess he won't be following me anytime soon.* He focused on his next victim. *Master Sergeant, sir, you're so dead.*

The snow was now blanketing his windshield with thick wet snow so he turned on his windshield wipers. He kept his focus on the main road directly ahead.

As he turned right onto the main road, he heard more sirens coming up behind him and nervously stared into his rearview mirror. "Not the damn cops again," he cursed and reached inside his jacket toward his holster. Stepping on the accelerator he tried to race ahead of the sirens that were now right behind him. He pulled over and noticed the ambulance turned down the dirt road heading toward Griffin's house.

Silas relaxed after the ambulance disappeared from

sight and released his death grip on the steering wheel. He closed his eyes for a few moments, suddenly overcome with fatigue. He realized that he needed to grab some sustenance and shut eye, so drove down the main road toward the nearest motel. Tomorrow he would get an early start for his trip to Vermont.

CHAPTER 21
(Friday, March 4, 2016) 9:15 a.m.

Trace, Sheila, and the officer stood in the pale morning light, somberly staring at the charred remains of what had once been Jake's family's house. Each was silently wondering what secrets the house would reveal. One secret had already been divulged by Sheila shortly after they arrived at the scene, a few minutes behind Trace and the officers.

Sheila held a manila envelope in her hands and walked over to Trace. She informed Trace and the officers that the Fire Investigator found a can of gasoline lying on the ground near where the front entrance used to be and found traces of gasoline resin at various locations on pieces of burned wood. Sheila handed the envelope to Trace and replied, "He confirmed that the fire was started by gasoline and was intentional." Trace briefly glanced up from reading the report she removed from the envelope and nodded at her. "More compelling evidence for our case," she declared.

Sheila turned toward Ramsey standing next to Trace and continued her report. "Oh, by the way, Officer, I spoke with a ballistics expert yesterday about the casings you found in Silas' trench coat, and they match the ones we found here." Ramsey smiled at Berryman and smugly replied, "As I thought."

Trace and the officers slowly walked around the blackened wooden posts, surveying what was left of the house. An acrid, sooty odor scorched their noses and billowing smoke filled their lungs.

Trace coughed and carefully stepped her way through piles of hot ashes, twisted plastic remnants, and crushed beer cans. She shuddered to think about how much hatred at one time filled the house and eventually burned it to the ground. Shreds of details of the police reports she read the previous evening came to mind. She recalled reading about Jake's war injuries, and the descriptions of him as angry, hostile, and violent. She read about Silas' past history and how he struggled in school and had difficulty making friends. She recalled reading all the documentation of suspected domestic abuse and wondered why no action was ever taken against Jake. She knew beyond a shadow of a doubt it was Jake who killed Martha, yet he was clever enough to disguise his heinous deed as accidental.

Like father, like son, she wryly smiled at the thought. Every bit of information was another piece of the puzzle put in place to solve the mystery of the man known as Silas Samuels.

Trace looked around and saw Murray and Ramsey doing their own investigations a few feet away from where she stood. She noticed Tomlinson and Sheila were watching them from outside the burned-out house.

Surveying the dust and fire scoured remnants that surrounded her, another area caught her attention. The area appeared to be concrete and just past it she observed the remnants of wooden floor boards barely covering a small pit where dirt was pushed away. She cautiously approached the area and stepped down into the dirt pit. She saw what appeared to be whitish objects that were laying at the bottom of the pit. Staring down at the objects, she let out a small gasp at the realization of her discovery.

Kneeling down, she pulled out and donned a pair of gloves from her tote bag. She picked up the bone fragments and studied them for a few moments. One resembled a human finger or toe bone, and another fragment appeared round, similar to the top covering of a skull. Upon closer inspection, she noticed a bullet hole penetrated the surface of the bone. She instantly started digging in the area with her fingers and pulled several more bone fragments from the ashes and dirt.

Trace called out to Murray and Ramsey who walked over to where she knelt. Tomlinson and Berryman stopped their conversation and followed close behind the officers. She showed them her findings, and after donning their gloves, they examined the bones. Murray held up the skull fragment and gazed at the bullet hole. Trace looked over at Tomlinson and Berryman and pointed toward the fragments they were holding. "You might want to give these to forensics, especially this one." She pointed toward the skull fragment that Murray was examining. "This one is pretty clear evidence of what happened to Jake."

Berryman smiled and nodded toward Trace. "Good finding, Detective. It's always good to have extra eyes involved in a crime scene investigation.”

Tomlinson’s cell rang and after answering the call, he handed his bone fragments to Berryman. “Hey, Sergeant. What’s up?” As he talked with Sergeant Jacobs his facial expression turned solemn. After a few minutes of conversation with Sergeant Jacobs, he turned to face the officers. “Jacobs just received a report of another murder in the Adirondacks. The officer that found Joe Griffin informed her that he died while en route to the hospital. The officer and paramedics did CPR, but they couldn’t revive him.”

They all stood staring at Tomlinson in shocked silence for a few moments. Murray was the first to speak. “When did this happen?”

“Earlier this morning,” Tomlinson somberly replied.

Murray impatiently kicked his foot at a pile of dirt and ashes. “This guy needs to be stopped. We should get going,” he grumbled.

Trace stood with her arms folded over her chest and realized Murray was right. She knew that Nielson would be Silas’ next target in Vermont, yet felt inept standing at a crime scene in another state. She thought about Dan and wished he were there with her.

Ramsey’s voice interrupted her thoughts. “Ready, Detective?” Ramsey glanced at her momentarily and waited for her reply.

Letting out a long sigh, she nodded. She extended her hand and thanks to Berryman and Tomlinson. “Please keep us informed about the forensics report on our findings today and any other information you receive.”

Berryman smiled at her. “Thanks again, Detective. We

will submit this new evidence to forensics and will certainly notify you of their findings and keep in communication."

Tomlinson tipped his hat toward Trace. "Until we meet again, Detective."

As Trace hurried away with Murray and Ramsey toward their squad car, she realized she needed to connect with Dan and warn him about Nielson.

Dan stood shivering on the front porch of Gina's house wearing only a thin wool jacket and wool knit pants. He recalled the events of the morning while waiting for someone to open the door. George had called earlier in the day to let him know they were home from the hospital and shared the good news that little Lynette was improving. Gina called after George's call to invite him over for lunch.

He was also finally able to connect with Nielson and they talked about Silas for most of the conversation. Nielson told Dan that the local police department already had surveillance officers patrolling his neighborhood. Dan felt unsettled and on edge after their conversation, knowing he had to face Silas again to settle the score. He knew he was only an hour drive away from Brightport and planned to leave early the next morning. He also wondered how he would update Gina and Wes on the current events, realizing this might be his last visit with them.

A light, wet snow fell as he hurriedly made the ten minute walk from his cabin to her house. Gina peeked out the front room window of her light blue and grey manufactured house and smiled at the sight of her brother. Rushing to the door, she gave Dan a big bear hug and ushered him into the house.

As they entered the brightly lit front room, Dan was greeted with the delicious smell of her homemade chicken vegetable soup. Harley rushed up to greet Dan by jumping on him with her trim black and white tail wagging excitedly. Dan smiled as always at the sight of Harley and reached down to scratch her furry head. "Hey, there, pal. Are you glad to see me?"

"We all are," Gina exclaimed and reached for Dan's jacket to hang on the coat rack next to the door. Wes also greeted Dan with a handshake and hearty clap on the back.

Wes ushered Dan over to the maple, brown frame sofa with grey and blue striped cushions, next to the window. The two men sat and chatted while Gina hurried into the kitchen to check on the soup. After a few minutes, she announced lunch was ready. Dan and Wes walked into the dining room and sat in wooden straight back chairs at the small mahogany wood table.

As they ate lunch, Dan caught them up with all the latest happenings since their last meeting the previous week. Dan mentioned visiting Annie and Gina interjected.

"We visited Annie several times since last week, and know about her pneumonia. She tells us she's been having dreams about a man who's trying to hurt her," Gina stated.

Dan stared at her wide-eyed. "You haven't told her about Peggy and Stephanie, have you?"

"No, of course not. Please give me more credit than that. I know this is a serious issue and I'm not going to interfere. Perhaps, it would be helpful if she talks with a counselor about her dreams."

Dan solemnly nodded. "I already talked with Dr. Wilson about this. He feels that before pursuing that route, she needs to recover from the pneumonia." Gina agreed.

Dan continued to update them with stories about his trip with Trace up to Lakeland to visit George and Susan.

"I just got off the phone with George, and he informed me little Lynette is improving. She is now able to breathe on her own and has been taken off life support. He said they might be able to take her home next week."

Wes smiled and declared, "We've been wondering what's happening with them and their baby, and are glad to hear this news."

Gina sighed. "We've been watching the news and we try to stay up to date with what's happening. Every time we turn on the TV, we hear about more victims. We've kept in contact with Sheriff Anderson, and he tells us that Samuels is still at large so he's still working on the case, yet that's all we ever hear," Gina declared between mouthfuls of soup.

Dan glanced up at Gina from his soup bowl and held his spoon in midair. "A lot has happened since his last visit almost two weeks ago. Detective Malone has been busy as of late and hasn't really had much time to update him on current events."

"I'll bet she's got a full plate trying to apprehend this murderer," Gina agreed.

Dan's phone came to life once again. Looking at his phone, he smiled. "Hey, Detective, we were just talking about you. I'm with Gina and Wes having lunch. What's up?"

"Dan, glad I caught you. I'm with my associates, Officers Murray and Ramsey, and we made a stop in Pines, Pennsylvania. We're now heading for the Adirondacks. Have you heard anything from Nielson?"

It's good to hear her voice again, yet there's something

"Yeah, I just talked with him yesterday. He said the local police in Brightport, Vermont are aware of his situation and have his neighborhood on surveillance. I'm planning on leaving early tomorrow morning to be there in case he gets a visit from an uninvited guest. It's about an hour away from Archer."

"Dan, please get there ASAP and be careful. I talked with Randolph, the detective who is working with George." She filled him in on all the details of Silas' work at the underground hacking organization. "So, I'm sure he knows that Nielson is now living in Brightport."

Dan pondered her last statement for a few moments.

"Yeah, you're right, Detective. I'm sure those records are kept updated. I was wondering how Silas knew where we all lived. I recall exchanging phone numbers with the members of our squad after training, yet I'm sure some numbers have changed over the past fifteen years, including mine. So, it makes sense that he hacked into our personal military records to find us."

Trace paused for a few moments to find the right words to inform Dan about Griffin.

"Dan, I want you to know that the uninvited guest visited Griffin as anticipated. I'm sure Griffin put up one hell of a fight, yet I'm sorry to report that Silas once again prevailed."

"Oh, God... no!" he slammed his hand down on the table. Gina and Wes stared at him, startled at his outburst.

Dan got up from the table and walked into the front room to continue the conversation with more privacy. There was a long pause and silence on the other end of the phone. Dan angrily paced around the front room.

"Dan, I wish I had better news. Are you okay?"

Dan finally found his voice. "I tried to warn him. Where in hell were the police? I thought he was under police surveillance!"

"Not yet knowing all the details, it's hard for me to tell you exactly what went down. He was under police surveillance, yet apparently Silas got to him before the officers did. The officer that found him tried to revive him, and the paramedics did CPR, yet he died before they could get him to the hospital. I'm sorry, Dan."

After another long pause, Dan tried to calm himself.

"I'm also sorry, Detective. I didn't mean to lash out at you. I know you've got enough on your plate right now. Trace, I swear, I will kill him myself! Silas needs to die!"

"Dan, I'm with you on that. Please try to calm down. We'll get him!"

Dan sat down on one of the recliners and gazed out the window at the steadily falling snow. As he reflected on all the events of the past two weeks, he wondered when it would end. His mission was crystal clear. *I refuse to let Silas claim another victim. Not on my watch! Silas will pay for his crimes with his life,* he vowed.

Watching the falling snow reminded him of happier times spent with Peggy and his daughters. It was too easy to succumb to sadness. He settled for a deeper and more insistent hunger to avenge the murders of his family and friends.

"Thanks, Detective, for reminding me of that fact." He recalled Trace mentioned she was in Pines, Pennsylvania earlier in their conversation. "What went down in Pines?"

"Ok, so Pines is where Silas and his family lived. Silas

paid a visit to his dad, Jake, and from the looks of the house, it didn't go well for his dad. He shot him and burned down the house."

"So, it sounds like there's a bit of family history between him and his dad."

"Yeah, definitely history with Jake, and his mother, Martha, as well. Apparently, Jake killed Martha and Silas was witness to this. He was also abused by his dad. So, his intention was pretty obvious."

"You're right, Detective. It's evident that he had family and other issues."

Dan heard some male voices in the background and car doors opening and closing over the phone.

"Dan, we're here at Adirondacks Headquarters, so I'm gonna get going. I'll call you when I get a chance. In the meantime, safe travels."

"You as well, Detective."

After giving Trace Nielson's address, Dan disconnected the call and stood in the front room staring out the window. Gina slowly approached her brother and wrapped her arm around his back. They stood together gazing out the window.

"More bad news?" she inquired.

Dan slowly nodded. He tried to find the words to tell her what he needed to do. "Gina, I need to take a road trip and I may not return."

Gina turned and gazed up at her brother with tears spilling down her face. "I know," she whispered.

CHAPTER 22
(Friday, March 4, 2016) 5:15 p.m.

Trace, Murray, and Ramsey were greeted by several officers at Adirondacks Police Headquarters, and a barrage of news reporters. Several reporters from a local news station ran up to Trace and the officers and showered them with questions about the murder of Joe Griffin.

"Do you know Mr. Samuels' whereabouts?" one woman reporter asked.

"We don't know his current whereabouts, but we do know he's heading to Vermont," one officer impatiently responded.

"What's being done to apprehend him?" another reporter persisted.

Trace looked directly into the camera and announced, "Wherever you are, Silas, we will find you." She waved away the relentless reporters firing questions at her and rushed up the steps outside of the Police Headquarters building.

One of the officers, Sergeant Rogers, led them back to a conference room, and introduced them to the Chief Officer, Brian Taglioni.

Taglioni was a large man in his mid-forties, big in stature and wide in girth, with black curly hair and matching moustache. His very presence commanded attention and he expected no less. He wore a navy blue uniform, as did the officers he commanded, and when he stood to shake hands with Trace, Murray, and Ramsey, he breathed heavily. He greeted the officers with a thick New York accent. "Welcome to the State of New York. I wish it were under different circumstances. Thanks, Officers and Detective, for your visit."

He waved them over to seats around the conference table. Sergeant Rogers joined them at the table and they all took their seats. Rogers began the conversation.

"So, we heard you were just visiting Pines and saw the house where the Samuels family used to live. We also heard about what went down there per Sgt. Jacobs. We know that Samuels has been focusing his vengeance on his squad mates, and in this case, Joe Griffin."

Trace nodded. "Before we get started, I'd like to add that right now our main priority is Master Sergeant Nielson. Silas, or Samuels, or Stuart Wyatt, as per his fake ID, is probably heading for Nielson's home in Brightport, Vermont as we speak."

Taglioni leaned forward on his folded arms. "Let me assure you, Detective, I personally alerted the Brightport Police Department first thing this morning. I realize this situation is of the utmost urgency and that Nielson's life is at stake. That's where I come in, to make sure that things get done in a timely fashion, you might say."

Trace breathed a sigh of relief and thanked Taglioni.

She also updated him and Rogers on her conversation with Randolph on their drive from Pines.

Taglioni nodded. "Interesting, Detective. We were wondering how he found his victims. Any more news on this company?" Trace shook her head and stated she would keep him posted. He signaled to Sergeant Rogers who walked over to the detective and officers and placed a manila envelope on the table in front of them.

"These are Griffin's crime scene photos. The officer who found him bound and gagged tried to revive him, as the paramedics also did, yet by the time he reached the hospital, he was pronounced dead," he explained.

Murray and Ramsey looked at a few photos and asked the officer a few questions, yet Trace was somewhere else in her mind.

As they studied the photos, Trace suddenly felt a wave of revulsion rush through her body. Turning her head away from the photos, she gazed out the window and noticed it was already dark outside. She wondered, *What's wrong with me? It's not the photos that I can't deal with. I've seen plenty of gory crime scene photos, yet I'm done here!* She couldn't stop thinking about Dan and wanted to be with him. She thought about all the trauma inflicted by Silas' murderous mission of revenge, and she wanted to put an end to him and the violence once and for all.

Murray's voice interrupted her thoughts. "Anything wrong, Detective?" She turned her head around and noticed

Murray and Ramsey looking at her with concern on their faces. She met their gaze straight on.

"No, I'm fine. It's late and I think we're done here," she declared as she stood and grabbed her tote bag. She calmly collected the photos from Murray and Ramsey and handed them back to Rogers. All the officers and Taglioni stared at her like she was an alien from another planet.

Composing herself, she faced the officers and spoke from a place of centeredness and rationality.

"As I previously mentioned, there's nothing more that can be done here. I feel my place is now back in Vermont with my client, Dan, and Master Sergeant Nielson. I swear to you, as sure as I am still standing, that Silas will either share the same fate of all his innocent victims or be brought to justice!"

She waved to Murray and Ramsey. "Come on guys, we have more pressing work to do and tracks to make." Chief Taglioni stood up and walked toward her and the officers.

"Detective, I admire your determination and guts. I understand your need to find Samuels and put an end to his madness. I wish you good luck and reiterate we're here for backup."

Trace said her thanks to Taglioni and Rogers and requested that a copy of the photos be sent to her office. They all shook hands and said their goodbyes. She nodded toward Murray and Ramsey, and they followed her out the conference room door and left the station.

As they headed toward their vehicle, Murray smiled at Trace. "Detective, you sure know how to captivate an audience," he teased. Ramsey chuckled appreciatively.

She smiled at his comment. "Yep, just another one of

my many talents," she poked her elbow good naturedly into his arm. Letting out a long sigh, she remarked, "It's been a long day, fellas. How about we grab some fast food and then hit the road? Hopefully, we can beat Silas back to Vermont."

CHAPTER 23
(Friday, March 4 – Saturday, March 5, 2016)

Silas wearily entered the motel wearing his tan baseball cap and green camouflage jacket. He pulled the cap forward in an attempt to hide his battered face. In his hand, he held a bag of Chinese food he had picked up on the way to the motel. He checked in with the middle aged front desk clerk who eyed him suspiciously as he approached her. She checked his ID and somewhat taken aback by his appearance, asked him what happened.

Nervously smiling, he explained, "I had a minor skirmish with some obnoxious guy in a bar. You think this looks bad, well, you should see him!" The woman snorted at his bad joke, pointed to the elevator and handed him the keys to his room on the second floor.

Silas left the elevator and wearily trudged down the hall toward his room. Entering his room, he turned on the foyer light and walked into the bathroom to attend to his wounds. Glancing in the mirror, he stood with his mouth agape as he observed his swollen face and nose. Touching his nose, he winced in pain. *I hope it's not broken,* he thought. He examined his left shoulder and right leg and perceived the wounds were superficial, although still painful.

Silas wearily sat on the bed in his motel room and hungrily ate his Chinese takeout right from the carry out box. Even though it was only 8 p.m., he felt exhausted from lack of sleep. All the events of the chaotic past few days were playing repeatedly in his mind like a broken record.

He remembered the officers pursuing him earlier that evening after offing Griffin, and he smiled at the thought. *Griffin got what he deserved and so did all my other victims,* he thought. *Especially you, Dad. Ah, yes, revenge is indeed sweet!*

He knew he still needed to deal with Nielson, yet savored this moment of satisfaction like a spider playing with a fly caught in its web before making its final fatal attack. He recalled Nielson visiting him in the hospital in Afghanistan, and he could even hear his words as clearly as though the conversation occurred just yesterday. "You're in a lot of trouble, Samuels." The words echoed in his mind, and he pictured Nielson standing next to him as he spoke. *I hate to be the bearer of bad tidings, sir, but you're in a lot of trouble as well, sir!* He maliciously grinned and brought his hand to his head in a mock salute to the Master Sergeant.

Silas planned to leave the next morning after he got some sorely needed shut eye. *After all, it was only a three hour drive from the Adirondacks to Brightport,* he reasoned. *He* found the remote lying next to him in bed and turned on the

TV. He watched only part of a bad thriller movie and soon fell into a deep slumber.

Silas awoke with a start sometime around 2:30 a.m. *Was I having a bad dream again?* he wondered. Half asleep, he noticed he was still fully clothed and lying on top of his neatly made bed. Somewhere in the distance, he heard the voice of a news reporter coming from the TV in his room that was still on.

"The East Coast killer, Silas Samuels, claimed yet another victim, Joe Griffin, a few days ago." Silas sleepily stared at his photo shown on the screen, yet something else he heard from the reporter caught his attention.

"…We already know he is now driving a silver Camaro and is using a fake ID under the guise of Stuart Wyatt. As with our previous reports, we now know his attacks are mainly centered on former members of his squadron and that his next target is William Nielson. We have learned that the Brightport police have been alerted and they have surveillance teams patrolling the area…"

Just as he was ready to reach for the remote, a woman's face appeared on the screen and he recognized her. The reporter introduced her as Detective Malone, and her closing words echoed in his mind. "Wherever you are, Silas, we will find you."

Now wide awake, Silas changed his plans and decided to leave in the darkness to reduce the risk of being noticed. Luckily, the desk clerk wasn't the same lady who checked him in. The attractive young lady clerk smiled at him as he checked out. "Goodnight, Mr. Wyatt, and have a great evening."

"You as well," he slyly smiled at her and hurried outside to the parking lot where his silver chariot awaited him. *She obviously hasn't watched the news lately,* he chuckled to himself. He turned off the obscene thoughts in his mind about the young desk clerk, and focused on Nielson, his last target.

Reaching his Camaro, he drove off toward Highway I 87 North, and after a coffee stop at a gas station made his way toward Brightport.

As he drove, his mind was once again filled with thoughts and images of Detective Malone. Silas looked forward to encountering her again. *She was pretty good for a girl,* he thought, *yet no match for an ex-marine.*

Holding his coffee cup in the air he toasted her and smiled. "This one's for you, Detective!"

CHAPTER 24
(Saturday, March 5, 2016) 5:30 a.m.

Covered with cold sweat and breathing heavily, Silas sat in his vehicle hidden behind some thick bushes overlooking an open meadow a few hundred feet across from Nielson's property. Scanning the area, he detected a squad car parked in the long paved driveway of the two story house. He saw an officer walking around the perimeter of the house about a hundred feet from where he was parked. Another squad car pulled up and an officer got out. Silas noticed he was wearing a silver badge on his cap and jacket, and surmised he was of a high rank, either Lieutenant or Captain.

The two officers approached each other and were involved in conversation, standing with their backs toward Silas.

Making his move, he grabbed his Beretta from his holster and quietly opened the door of his Camaro. He reached down to pick up a rock lying on the ground, and he flung the rock toward the officers. It flew over their heads and landed with a thud a few feet away from where they stood. They stopped dead in their tracks and focused their attention on the object. The Captain signaled to the other officer and he ran toward the object to investigate.

Silas silently crept toward them. He stood behind a tree holding his breath and contemplated his next move. The Captain signaled to the other officer and he ran toward the back of Nielson's house and disappeared from sight. Seeing his chance, Silas rushed up to the Captain and delivered a sharp blow to the back of his head with the butt of his Beretta. The officer silently slumped to the ground.

Silas quickly dragged his limp body through the forest back to his car and he hoisted him into the back seat. He immediately went to work and pulled the two way radio off the officer. He got back in the driver's seat and listened to the sounds coming from the radio. He heard voices interspersed with static pouring from the radio. "Captain, come in, Captain Gregory… Silas pushed the side button and spoke into the radio. "Gregory here." He nervously paused waiting for the reply.

"Captain, I just wanted to report that everything looks good on this end."

Silas thought fast. "Okay. Same here. I just got word from the Deputy Chief that our surveillance has been cancelled until further notice. He wants us to return to the precinct." Silas held his breath as he anticipated the reply.

He heard static and then the officer's voice came back. "Copy that, Captain. Was there any reason given?"

Silas tried to hold his voice steady and sound convincing. "Yes. I was informed that new surveillance officers will be heading over later this morning to relieve us. As of now, we're officially off duty. I'll meet you back at the precinct after I greet the new officers."

There was a pause and more static. "Okay, copy that, sir. Over and out."

Silas surveyed the perimeter of the two story house and within five minutes, he noticed the other officer was walking toward his squad car. He got in and drove down the road past where Silas' car was parked.

Silas watched the car turn toward the main road and disappear from sight. He breathed a sigh of relief and glanced behind him at the Captain lying unconscious on the back seat and bleeding from his head wound. "Sorry about the knock on the head, sir, but you're not needed at the present moment."

After he bound and gagged the Captain, he got out of the car and slowly walked toward Nielson's house. He studied the two-story house for a few moments. It was long and narrow, yet extended some forty feet back. The house was completely dark with all windows covered by wooden shades.

He approached the front entrance, and listened for signs of movement in the house, yet heard nothing except the sound of the chilling wind whipping around him. Peering in the wooden sash windows, he saw only silhouettes of tall lamps perched atop front room tables. He tried turning the front doorknob, yet as he expected, it was locked. Trying his lock release gun on the deadbolt lock proved futile. *I wonder if it's a six pin tumbler?* He shined his flashlight on the doorknob and seeing the name Schlage on the lock confirmed his suspicion.

Glancing over to his left, he noticed a white stone footpath that led around the side to the back of the house. Silas followed the path that led to the back entrance and walked up the three wooden steps to the back porch.

He approached the white framed door and gently opened the screen door. It creaked as it opened and Silas paused for a few moments, hoping that Nielson wouldn't hear the noise. He pulled out his lock release gun from his jacket pocket, expecting the door to be locked. To his surprise, the door easily opened.

Silas walked into the kitchen and looked around. Walking past a small sized island countertop in the middle of the kitchen, he noticed the room smelled of apple-scented dish soap and the tantalizing, lingering odor of fresh cooked turkey. Licking his lips at the thought of food, he proceeded into the dining room, and walked past the rectangle dark wood table that led toward the front room.

In the master bedroom upstairs, Nielson awoke from a sound sleep with a start. *What was that noise I heard? It sounded like the screen door creaking.* Gazing over at the alarm clock on the nightstand, he noticed it read 6:05 a.m.

He lie on his back staring at the ceiling and listening for any more sounds. He only heard silence. He expected Dan's arrival sometime in the afternoon. He also knew that his wife, Cheryl, was staying with a neighbor for a few days and the kids were staying overnight with their friends. He breathed a sigh of relief knowing they were safe, yet he felt especially alone and vulnerable knowing that Silas was on the loose. But, he was prepared for Silas.

He got up out of bed and quickly dressed in old combat fatigues and a t-shirt. Reaching for his 44 Magnum lying on the nightstand, he slowly opened the bedroom door and peered out into the hall. He slowly and silently crept into the hall holding his weapon in front of him. *Just like old times,* he thought and steeled himself at the thought of confronting Silas.

Standing in front of his bedroom, he glanced to his left and right at the double sided staircase that led down to the main floor and wondered which one would be his escape route. Realizing the staircase to his left led to the kitchen where the back door was located, he decided to avoid that area. He descended the staircase to his right that led to the front room.

Silas stood in the front room and noticed a staircase leading to the upstairs bedrooms, and walked past it. He walked toward the kitchen and headed up another staircase. As he approached the upper landing, he reached inside his holster, pulled out his Beretta, and slowly headed down the hall toward the master bedroom.

Nielson made his way downstairs into the front room and scanned the room searching for Silas. He heard a creaking of the floorboards above him and stopped dead in his tracks. He felt his heart pounding inside his chest and glanced up in the direction of the master bedroom where he was only five minutes prior. *He's probably in there right now,* he thought. Remembering the officers patrolling outside, he looked out a nearby window and noticed one lone patrol car was still parked in the driveway.

Nielson allowed himself to feel comforted at the sight and let out a short breath of relief. Determined to rid himself of Samuels once and for all, he turned and ascended the same staircase he had previously descended.

Holding his Magnum in front of him, he paused momentarily at the top landing and silently crept down the hallway and turned to his left facing the master bedroom. Holding his breath, he turned the doorknob and slowly opened the door a crack. He stood in the doorway and kicked the door wide open. With adrenaline coursing through his body, he flipped on the light switch and charged into the room. His eyes wildly darted around the room and sweat poured profusely down his face.

"Okay, Samuels," he yelled to an empty room. Show your damn face!" Hearing a noise behind him, he swung around to find himself standing face to face and gun to gun with Silas standing in the doorway.

"Well, we finally meet at last Master Sergeant, sir. You haven't changed a bit," Silas sneered and stood his ground. Nielson met Silas' sinister gaze and felt an intense hatred pouring from his eyes. They stood in an impasse for a few minutes that seemed like an eternity to Nielson.

"You either. Have you looked at yourself lately? You look like hell, Samuels!"

Silas shifted his weight and his mouth curled into a mocking smirk. "With all due respect, sir, I have been through the gates of hell and back since you put me there!"

"You deserved it Samuels, for deserting your squadron when they needed you most."

Silas could barely contain his rage. "I saved Morris' life, but there was very little in court mentioned about that fact!"

"You got off easy because of that fact, Samuels. You're

lucky you didn't get worse!"

Silas leaned forward toward Nielson and inched his Beretta closer toward his forehead. "Put the gun down, now!"

Nielson slowly shook his head and stood his ground, pointing his gun toward Silas.

A deep male voice behind Silas distracted him. "Now, you put the gun down, Silas, nice and slow." The officer stood a few feet behind Silas pointing the barrel of his gun at the back of Silas' head.

CHAPTER 25
(Saturday, March 5, 2016) 5:45 a.m.

Dan said his farewells to Gina, Wes and Harley, and was on the road to Brightport by 5:45 a.m.

As he drove, he thought about seeing Nielson again after fifteen years, and wondered if he had changed any. He pictured Nielson with his tall, slim build and crewcut. He recalled that when he was still in the Marines, he never really had much time to know Nielson during their time spent in Afghanistan. He knew that Nielson had married while still in the service and that his wife was named Cheryl.

He recalled from his last phone call a year ago that Nielson became a pilot after leaving the Marines and had recently started his own business as a charter pilot. He spent most of his time flying military personnel to various parts of the country. Nielson told Dan that he had two children, Julie and Justin, who were ten and twelve at the time. Dan also knew

Nielson was a baseball fan and spent his free time volunteering as a little league coach.

When Nielson called Dan last night, he mentioned he made sure Cheryl and the children wouldn't be there when Dan arrived. He said Cheryl was visiting with a neighbor and the kids were staying over at their friend's house. *Probably good they weren't involved, in light of Nielson's situation,* he thought.

As he got closer to Nielson's house, he remembered his conversation last night with Trace and her promise to call him. *I wonder if she got back home alright?*

Glancing at his dashboard, he noticed the time was now 6:40 a.m. He decided to call and dialed her number, but there was no answer. He left a message and wondered where she was. *Maybe she was already en route to Nielson's house… Maybe she's still asleep. She was putting in lots of miles over the past few days driving from Pennsylvania to the Adirondacks and then back to Waterton. I wonder if her partners, Murray and Ramsey, will be accompanying her to Nielson's house?*

Gazing out the driver's side window, he noticed he was passing a large lake and recreation area, and was immediately filled with memories of past camping experiences there with Peggy and the girls. Feelings of familiar sadness were now overwhelming him. His eyes filled with tears at the memories, and he tried to push them out of his mind.

He tried Trace's number again and this time she answered.

"Hey Dan, sorry I didn't answer…" her voice sounded faint and far away. "I'm drinking coffee and trying to wake up."

He smiled at the thought of her lying in bed and secretly wished he were lying next to her.

No, don't go there, he reprimanded himself. *You're still grieving the loss of Peggy and Stephanie! Am I falling for her? How could it be? What am I thinking? It's only been a few weeks. Maybe I'm just trying to find a replacement for Peggy, yet no! There's no replacing her,* he thought, yet something about Trace also tugged at his heart. *I definitely have feelings for her...*

Trace's sleepy voice brought him back to their conversation.

"What time is it?"

"It's 6:45 a.m., Detective. Time to get rolling. Remember, we have a date with Nielson."

"I didn't get to bed until after midnight and couldn't fall asleep. It was about 10 p.m. when Murray and Ramsey dropped me off at home before they headed back to the precinct to do paperwork. I called Jennie and found out she's not pregnant, thank God. She says she's been seeing a therapist and she feels it's helping her deal with her attack and Sean's death."

"Glad to hear that she's doing better. Any further news to report?"

"Yeah, it's been an interesting last few days. I'm sure we'll have plenty of time to catch up when I get to Nielson's. I'm already on the road. By the way are you there yet?"

Dan glanced out the window and noticed he was entering a wooded area overlooking a nearby lake. "I'm almost there. I'd better let you go to pay attention here."

"Be safe, okay? I hope you have your gun with you. I'll see you within the next hour."

"Yes, I do. Be safe yourself, Detective, and safe travels."

Dan parked the car in an open meadow directly across from Nielson's house and reached for his Smith & Wesson laying on the passenger seat. As he stared out the window, he noticed the skies were dark grey, signaling an approaching snowstorm. He saw a light sprinkling of snow was starting to fall.

He remembered Nielson saying that surveillance officers were patrolling the area. Scanning the perimeter of the house, he saw two patrol cars parked on the driveway, but didn't see any officers on patrol. He heard only dead silence.

CHAPTER 26
(Saturday, March 5, 2016) 6:03 a.m.

The officer drove slowly down the road leading from Nielson's house with a weird feeling in the pit of his stomach. He recalled his conversation with the Captain and he thought, *something wasn't right about the Captain. It didn't sound like the Captain's voice,* and he wondered why he gave an order to leave the area immediately when they had only started their shift a half hour ago?

As he drove, his eyes focused on a small building that resembled a shed off in the forest to his right. He squinted his eyes to adjust to the light from his headlights, and he noticed part of a silver car bumper partially hidden behind the shed and surrounding trees.

He parked the squad car along the side of the road and got out to investigate. Approaching the car with his flashlight, he noticed the car was a Camaro, and recognized it from news and police report briefings as the car Silas Samuels was driving. He shone the flashlight into the car and realized it was the Captain sitting upright and staring in his direction. He tried opening both passenger and driver side doors, but they were locked. Running back to his squad car, the officer returned with a window punch tool and signaled for the Captain to lie back down on the seat. Smashing the glass of the driver's side window with the punch, he gained entrance to the car.

After freeing the Captain from the duct tape bonds around his hands and mouth, the Captain thanked him. "I knew that your voice sounded different, but I attributed it to all the static on the radio," the officer apologized. The Captain nodded at the officer. "I'm glad you came back." After a short discussion, they raced back to the house in to apprehend Silas.

Feeling the gun barrel pointing at his head, Silas sprang into action. He fired his Beretta at Nielson's shooting arm, knocking him and his gun to the floor. Silas quickly dove to the floor and fired several shots at the man behind him who he discovered was a police officer.

Silas saw another officer, who he recognized as the Captain, running toward him and fired a shot at his chest. The Captain also fell to the floor.

Silas observed the officers now lying motionless on the floor in pools of blood. He slowly got up and walked over to the first man he shot, and flipped him over on his back. Staring down at the man, he recognized him as the officer who he spoke to on the radio when he cancelled the surveillance. *He probably came back to check on the Captain, who wasn't really the Captain,* he chuckled to himself.

Silas glanced into the master bedroom and observed Nielson crawling on his good hand and knees toward where his Magnum was laying on the floor. He rushed toward Nielson and delivered a swift kick to his side. Nielson let out a groan, clutching his side with his bloody right hand, and grabbed for Silas' foot with his good hand, pulling him down to the floor. Silas landed on his belly with a thud.

Nielson was now back on his feet and rushed over toward his Magnum a few feet from where Silas lay. As he bent over to pick up his gun, Silas flipped over on his back and turned to face Nielson. He kicked out at Nielson's backside and sent him pitching forward onto the floor. The Magnum once again slid out of his reach.

Silas staggered over to where Nielson lay beneath the two windows in the bedroom. He caught a brief glance of daylight filtering in through the halfway drawn window shades. He stood above Nielson's prone body and declared in a voice devoid of emotion, "Sorry, to report sir, that your time is up." He lifted his Beretta and pointed it at Nielson's head.

Nielson quickly turned on his side and scissor kicked Silas' legs. Silas fell backwards to the floor and landed on his back with a hard thud that left him gasping for air.

Nielson ran toward his Magnum and fired it at Silas, hitting his thigh. Silas grabbed his bloody thigh and cried out in pain. Nielson turned and fled down the stairs, dodging bullets from Silas' Beretta that ricocheted off the banister around him.

As he raced toward the front door, he passed the foyer hall closet where he kept his old arsenal of weapons when he served as a Marine. He tore open the closet door, opened the arsenal box, and quickly pulled out his M240 machine gun and hurried out the front door.

Glancing back over his shoulder, toward the front door, he saw no trace of Silas. He ran past the two empty squad cars sitting on his driveway, and he recalled seeing the two dead surveillance officers that Silas shot in the hallway outside his bedroom.

Nielson winced in pain as he clutched his wounded, bloody arm. He knew he had to get to a hospital to get the bullet removed, yet he had a more pressing contingency plan at the moment. *I need to make fast tracks outta here,* he thought. *Silas could be right on my heels!*

Just at that moment, a Mustang pulled up and he saw Dan get out of the car and approach the driveway. "Need a lift?" he heard Dan's familiar voice call to him.

Nielson broke into a sprint toward Dan's car, and signaled to Dan to get back in the car. "Let's go!" he yelled. Dan got the message and jumped over the hood of the car and swung himself back into the driver's seat. He opened the passenger door for Nielson and slowly pulled away from the driveway. Nielson dove into the seat and off they drove. He let out a sigh of relief and smiled at Dan. "Hey, man, it's good to see you again!" They shook hands while Nielson tried to catch his breath.

"Yeah, you're a sight for sore eyes as well," Dan chided.

They careened away from Nielson's house toward the main road in the midst of a heavy snowfall. As they drove, Nielson filled Dan in on what went down between him and Silas.

Dan queried, "Where's Silas now?"

"Last time I looked, he was lying on the bedroom floor after I shot him in the thigh. That's when I grabbed this baby and left the house." He held up his machine gun.

Dan glanced at Nielson and saw his bloodied arm and disheveled appearance and remembered his fight for his own life with Silas a few weeks prior.

"Hey, Nielson, looks like you better have your arm checked before you bleed to death. Glad I arrived when I did."

Nielson winced in pain and tried to smile at Dan. "Yeah, me as well."

"Can I drive you to the hospital?"

Nielson shook his head. "No, I've got a better idea." He pulled his cell phone from his pocket and made a call.

"Hey, Hank, this is Nielson. Do me a favor, okay? We're about fifteen to twenty minutes away. Have The Falcon ready for me. I'll explain later."

Dan stared at Nielson in bewilderment.

"What's up, man?" he asked.

Nielson let out a wicked laugh.

"We're gonna get that bastard!"

CHAPTER 27
(Saturday, March 5, 2016) 7:30 a.m.

Trace disconnected her call and sighed. She talked with Dan and couldn't understand half of what he was trying to tell her due to all the static and noise in the background. Dan mentioned he was with Nielson at the airport, yet the call was lost after that. *What were they doing there?* she wondered. She understood that Silas was still in Nielson's house, yet she missed the whereabouts part.

She stood at the back entrance of the house and opened the screen door, startled at the creaking sound. *That's not gonna work,* she chided herself.

Trace walked around the side of the house holding her semiautomatic directly in front of her. She approached a side window and backed up against the side of the house to hide her body from sight. Peering in the window, she saw the front room was empty. She tried the window, and it silently opened wide enough for her to slide inside.

Trace walked around the front room and studied her surroundings. She was in a huge modernly decorated room with a red and white brick fireplace in the middle of the room. Walking toward the fireplace, she looked to her right and observed a cream color sofa sitting in front of three large rectangular picture windows that offered sweeping views of the mountainous surroundings. There were two side rectangular windows flanking the three middle windows.

Trace noticed the side window she crawled through was still slightly ajar. She felt a cold breeze blowing in through the crack, and shivering, she quietly shut the window. To her right was the front foyer leading to the front entrance. To her left, was a dark Cherrywood staircase with white bannisters flanking the staircase.

Walking over to the staircase, she noticed the dining room and kitchen lie directly behind it. Glancing upstairs, she wondered where Silas was hiding. She listened for any sounds or clues that would alert her to his location. She made her way back to the sofa and hid behind it to bide her time.

Silas clutched his steadily bleeding thigh, hobbled toward the window of the master bedroom, and watched Nielson running down the driveway toward a car parked in the street. He saw him signal to the driver, and watched the car drive off down the street. He wondered who the driver was and where they were going. He squinted his eyes to see the face of the driver, but it was dark inside the car. He saw the car was a Mustang. He recalled the blue Mustang that was parked in the driveway a few weeks ago when he paid Dan a visit. *Perhaps*

Dan was taking him to a hospital or to the police station. Either way, they'll be back and with Dan will be Detective Malone, so I'll be prepared for them.

Backing away from the window, he deliberated his next move. He staggered out of the bedroom and into the hallway. He limped into the back bedroom and noticed a pair of windows next to a door that led out to the upstairs back porch. Gazing out one of the windows, he observed the roof directly above him and decided that he would wait there for Dan and Trace. *The roof will give me the best vantage point to watch for their arrival,* he thought.

Silas unlocked and opened the door and gingerly stepped outside onto the porch. Staggering toward the back of the porch, he hefted himself up onto the bannister. He crawled up to the roof, leaving a trail of blood behind him.

Trace heard a noise upstairs that sounded like a door closing and felt a familiar rush of adrenaline surge through her body. She heard another sound and realized it was the pounding of her heart.

Okay, Silas, the buck stops here... Trace held her semiautomatic in front of her and slipped out from behind the sofa. Scanning the front room, she hurried toward the staircase and ran upstairs taking two steps at a time.

She paused at the top landing and searched the hallway for any movement, swinging her semiautomatic from left to right. *There it was again, another noise, but this time it came from outside.*

She heard the loud whooshing sound of an aircraft flying over the house and it came from the direction of the back

bedroom. She also heard gunfire and the sound of bullets rico-
cheting off the ceiling above her, followed by footsteps running
across the roof.

In a flash, she sprinted down the hallway and into the
back bedroom. She stared out the window, transfixed at the
spectacle displayed before her eyes.

A helicopter was hovering above the roof about 200
feet away from her, and Dan was standing outside on one of the
landing skids. In one hand, he held Nielson's M240 machine
gun pointed toward the roof, and with his other hand he held
onto a strap protruding from the open side door. She noticed
the pilot was Nielson.

Trace focused her attention on the chopper outside and
noticed it flew back toward the front of the house where the
chimney protruded upward from the roof.

Her thoughts were suddenly interrupted by the sound of
gunfire at the front entrance and the slamming of the door.

Silas ran across the roof from the back porch area
toward the front of the house, fleeing from the shots fired from
the chopper hovering above and chasing him. Every few seconds, he turned and fired his gun up at Dan, missing him each
time.

Standing at the edge of the roof above the front room,
Silas looked around for a quick way to get down from the roof.
He noticed a drain pipe led down to the front entrance and hurried toward it. He slid down the pipe and noticed the chopper
was directly above where he stood. Dan leaned in as the chopper flew over the front entrance of the house and fired more
rounds of ammunition at Silas, who fired back. Silas quickly

turned and entered the house through the front door.

Trace exited the back bedroom and hurried down the hallway toward the staircase. Glancing down at the front room area, she didn't see any sign of Silas. Hearing footsteps approaching behind her, she felt a hand grab for her neck.

"So, sweetheart, we meet again." She felt Silas' hot breath against her neck.

Trace instantly grabbed his hand with hers and pushed her head back hard into his face. Wincing in pain, Silas lunged at her and knocked her off balance. They both tumbled down the staircase and landed on the front room floor at the foot of the stairs. Trace's semiautomatic fell out of her hand and slid a few feet away from the staircase.

Silas tried to hoist his body on top of Trace. She immediately sprang up to a standing position and lifting her knee, reached for his head and kneed his face. Silas staggered back a few steps and dropped his Beretta to the floor.

Trace raced to pick up her gun, but before she could reach it, Silas charged at her again. She swiftly swung around to face him, and as he ran toward her, she stuck her foot out into his raging path. Silas tripped and landed on his belly.

Suddenly, they heard the roar of the chopper's rotor blades flying directly over the front room where they stood, and Trace's attention was diverted toward the window. In a flash, Silas was on his feet and he charged at her, knocking Trace to the floor.

Trace kicked her foot at his hand, knocking his Beretta to the floor, followed by another kick to his groin. Roaring like a lion, he released his grip on her throat and reached for his aching groin.

Trace rolled to a sitting position, quickly stood, and ran to pick up her gun a few feet away. Silas stood and rushed toward her. He wrapped his arm in a choke hold around her neck and her gun again dropped from her hand. He dragged her toward the window facing outside where the chopper now hovered directly above the front entrance. Dan had a birds-eye view of Trace's predicament so he angrily grabbed his harness and strapped it around his lower torso.

Trace jabbed her elbow hard into Silas' solar plexus, and delivered another blow to his nose with her raised clenched fist. Silas yelped in pain and released his choke hold. "You bitch!" he yelled at her with blood pouring down his face. Silas once again lunged toward her and pushed her hard to the floor.

Nielson maneuvered the chopper a few hundred feet away from the house and did a full circle turn. He pushed the pedals with both feet and rushed toward the house at full throttle. Dan was now hanging suspended in midair in his harness from the chopper.

He rappelled down to the ground and after releasing himself from the harness cable broke into a full out sprint toward the window.

Trace heard the sound of glass shattering and looked toward the window. She saw Dan burst in through the window feet first with his gun aimed at Silas' head.

She heard a shot ring out and she saw the next few moments in slow motion. Silas blankly stared at her with blood pouring from a bullet hole that pierced his forehead. He pitched forward and landed at her feet with a hard, lifeless thud. Trace stood for a few moments staring down at his inert body lying on the floor below her. She wondered if he was really dead and pushed him over on his back with her foot. She slowly bent down to check his neck for a pulse and couldn't find one. She breathed a sigh of relief and declared, "It's finally over, Silas, and so are you."

Trace glanced over toward the window where Dan stood and saw Dan wave up toward the chopper where Nielson looked down at him. He waved back to Dan and they both gave each other the thumbs up sign. Nielson maneuvered his chopper upwards towards the sky, and flew off toward the airport helipad.

Dan stepped over Silas and rushed toward Trace. Smiling broadly, he placed his Magnum back inside his holster and held out his hands to Trace. She reached for his hands and stood up in front of him. He leaned in close toward her face and she felt the heat of his lips next to hers. Trace lifted her lips to meet his and surrendered to the force of his passionate kiss. Instantly, all the tension, angst, and heartache of their recent desperate ordeal melted away. They held each other in a long embrace and shed tears together as a release of all the death and destruction of the past two weeks.

After a few moments, they broke their embrace and stood face to face staring at one another. Dan again reached for her hands and gently held onto them.

"I shouldn't have done that, Detective, and I'm sorry. It's just that…" Dan paused searching for his words. "I'm grateful for all you've done for me and my family."

Trace put her finger up to his lips. "Dan, no apologies are necessary. I understand what you are trying to say, believe me. Let's just leave it at that."

They held each other's gaze for a few moments. Dan nodded and slyly smiled.

He leaned toward her and whispered in her ear, "By the way, you owe me one, Detective."

Trace smiled. "You're on, Corporal."

CHAPTER 28
(Saturday, March 19, 2016) 8:45 a.m.

Gina and Wes walked silently next to Dan as they hurried toward Archer Memorial Hospital to meet with Dr. Wilson. Dan carried a gift for Annie he had picked up the previous day.

Today was the day they were taking Annie home and Dan was filled with both excitement and trepidation. He was relieved that Annie had recovered from pneumonia, yet he knew the hardest part of her recovery was yet to come. His mind was filled with questions. *How was he going to explain to her about Peggy and Stephanie? How would she deal with their deaths? When would she be able to return to school, and would she even be able to concentrate on her schoolwork? Will I even be able to remember all these questions to ask Dr. Wilson?*

Dan recalled his meeting with Gina and Wes the previous day, and smiled at his sister's kind invitation to have him and Annie move in with them. Although he didn't want to impose, he thought that would be the best option, especially for Annie to be with her remaining family members.

Gina held onto Wes' arm as they approached the hospital and Dan walked next to Gina. They all entered the hospital and took the elevator up to the 6th floor where Dr. Wilson's office was located.

After a short wait in the reception area of his office, Dr. Wilson walked out to greet them. They shook hands and followed him back to his private office where they all took seats. Dr. Wilson smiled at them and began the conversation.

"I am happy to report that Annie is doing really well. She has made a complete recovery from pneumonia, and has even been walking around the floor visiting with other patients, and playing with other children in the playroom." He paused for a few moments and continued his assessment of Annie's situation.

His eyes focused on Dan. "Annie is a strong and intelligent young lady, and I have heard from staff members that she has been asking them many questions about the whereabouts of her mother and sister. As we previously discussed, in light of all the trauma she has endured, I have arranged for a grief counselor to meet with you and Annie today before you leave. I thought it would be easier to have her present when you discuss the very difficult topic of death with Annie."

Dan nodded and breathed out a sigh of relief. *At least I won't have to deliver the bad news alone,* he thought.

"Dr. Wilson, I also had some other questions. Is it a good idea to consider long term therapy? I know I still have nightmares about that fateful night, and I'm also grieving the

deaths of Peggy and Stephanie. I wonder if you have any rec-
ommendations for a counselor for me as well?"

Dr. Wilson nodded and smiled at Dan. "Of course, I
recommend that all family members attend family counseling.
As all of you know, deaths in families affects the whole family.
I believe this counselor deals with family therapy as well. You
can decide the arrangements when you meet with her."

"What's her name?"

"Her name is Helen Gordon and you will meet her
shortly."

Dr. Wilson rested his elbows on his desk and tapped
his fingertips together in thoughtful contemplation. "Dan, do
you have a place to stay? I don't think it would be a good idea
for you or Annie to return to your house where this situation
occurred."

Gina reached for her brother's hand and squeezed it.

"Dan is welcome to stay at our house for as long as he
needs."

Wes suddenly remembered something he meant to tell
Dan and his face lit up. He smiled and leaned over toward Dan.
"Yes, we will have a very full house." Dan glanced over at Wes
with a puzzled expression on his face.

"Well," he began and tried to look serious. Gina looked
over at him and they both smiled at each other. "It seems that
we're gonna have another addition to the family," he proudly
exclaimed.

Dan stared at Wes as though he had lost his mind.
"What? I thought you guys didn't want any kids."

Wes laughed. "We don't. Harley wasn't acting like her
usual hyper self, and we thought there was something wrong

with her. We took her to the vet a few days ago and found out she's pregnant."

Dan smiled at Wes. "Well, I'll be darned. So, I guess I'm gonna be an uncle. Just wait until Annie finds out. She loves staying with you guys, especially because of Harley."

Dr. Wilson interjected. "I think this is fortuitous for Annie. Having a puppy companion will keep her focused on something positive rather than dwelling on her losses."

There was a knock at the door and a tall, attractive, silver-haired woman wearing a sporty tan pantsuit, entered the office. She introduced herself as Helen Gordon and they all shook hands. Helen talked with them for a few minutes and explained her role in helping her clients navigate the grieving process. She patiently answered their questions and handed Dan her business card. Dan liked her calmness and outgoing personality.

As they prepared to leave the office, Dr. Wilson received a phone call, and put the call on hold. He stood and faced Dan, Gina, and Wes. "I need to take this call, but you'll be in good hands with Helen. She's a good resource. Call me if you need anything further."

They thanked him and after leaving the office, they escorted Helen down the corridor toward Annie's room.

Seeing her family, Annie ran toward them wearing a huge smile on her face. "Daddy, Daddy!" she exclaimed. Dan knelt down as Annie ran into Dan's waiting arms. After hugging Dan, she broke away and engaged Gina and Wes in a group hug.

Still smiling, she glanced over at the strange lady who stood next to Wes, and then turned her attention back to Dan.

"Who's she, Daddy? Are we ready to go home? The nurse helped me get dressed and got my backpack, and now I'm all ready to go!"

Dan smiled and studied his daughter for a few moments. She wore a pink lace trimmed dress that Dan didn't recognize, and her long auburn hair was tied into pigtails with matching pink ribbons. Her freckled face was beaming and Dan was suddenly overcome with emotion. *She's been through so much, and she looks so beautiful as did Peggy,* he thought. *How do I tell her that her mother and sister are dead?*

Annie's voice interrupted his thoughts. "Daddy, are you okay? Do you like my new dress? Auntie Gina gave it to me." She smiled up at Dan and pulled on his pants leg.

Dan bent down and gathered her into his arms. "Yes, sweetheart, Daddy is fine. I love your dress. It's beautiful and so are you." He smiled at Gina, thanked her, and walked over to Annie's bed and set her gently down. Dan sat down next to her on the bed, and he handed her the gift he brought. Helen, Gina and Wes followed them and pulled over chairs around the bed. They sat down and amusedly watched Annie doing serious damage to the giftwrap covering her gift. She pulled out the big brown teddy bear and excitedly hugged it to her chest. "Thanks so much, Daddy!" she exclaimed and flung her arms around Dan, teddy bear and all.

Lovingly gazing over at Annie with tears mixed with sadness and joy in his eyes, Dan replied, "Annie, Daddy has something to tell you and this nice lady, Helen, is going to help me."

Later that evening, Dan and Trace stood in the doorway

of his cabin staring up at a brilliant full moon shining above them. Dan turned his face toward Trace, and their eyes met. Reaching for her hand, he smiled. Trace saw a familiar tenderness in his eyes and her heart melted.

"I want to show you something, Detective." They walked together through the forest behind the cabin where he had lived for the past month.

They walked in silence for a few minutes before Dan spoke. "This is where I've been spending a lot of time since that fateful night a month ago. This place brings me tremendous peace and gives me solace and solitude amidst all the world's chaos."

Trace shivered in the chilly night air, yet the heat radiating from Dan's hand warmed her entire body. She breathed in the fresh pine smell and scanned the surrounding forest. She saw endless rows of barren oak and pine trees immersed in slivers of white moonlight and felt a sense of serenity settle in her heart. "I see where you're coming from. This place feels so peaceful and otherworldly."

As they walked, Dan recounted everything he could remember about the day. He mentioned the call from George informing him they had brought Lynette home from the hospital a few days ago and that they were doing well. He told Trace about his call to Nielson who was recuperating in the hospital from the surgery on his arm and reunited with Cheryl and his children. He also talked about his time spent with Annie and the counselor, and Gina and Wes.

Trace shared that she received a phone call earlier in the day from Berryman informing her of the forensic report findings on Jake Samuels. "It's no big surprise that the bullet casings from Silas' trench coat matched the casings found at his house. Jake was identified with the bones I found in the rubble of what used to be his house. He died from a gun shot wound to his head. I'm glad that chapter has ended."

Dan glanced over at Trace with an expression of relief on his face. "Ashes to ashes, Detective."

Dan halted their stroll and they stood facing each other in silence for a few moments. Trace noticed his pensive expression. "A penny for your thoughts," she softly whispered.

Dan stared at Trace and let out his breath in a long sigh. "I know this is gonna be a long slog for Annie and me, yet I feel relieved that we're surrounded by loving family and friends. I consider you as a good friend also."

Trace put her hand on Dan's arm and smiled at him. "I feel the same about you, Dan, and I'm honored to have had the chance to get to know you."

Dan studied her face for a few moments. "What do you see when you look at me, Detective?"

"I see a very sad, yet strong man. You have to know that over time things will settle back into place."

"When I look at you, Detective, I feel your warmth and genuine nature. You help me feel centered and grounded." Dan sighed again. "I feel cut in half right now, and I need space and time to heal those wounds before I can become whole again and commit to another person. I don't want to inflict those wounds on you. I hope you understand."

Trace softly patted Dan's arm. "I understand and appreciate what you're saying. I'm not ready to take on another relationship either at present, and have my own wounds to heal. I think you summed it up perfectly when you said you considered me as a friend. I think that's how we should leave it, as being friends without expectations."

Dan nodded and smiled at Trace. He reached for her hand on his arm and held it in his hand. "You're on, Detective." They stood together in the forest staring up at the luminous full moon, immersed in the moment and the promise of a new future ahead.

The End of the Beginning…

About the author

Donna currently lives in Pearce, Arizona, with her husband, Gary, and their faithful tripod companion, Cadbury.
Her first book,
FINDING MEDUSA: THE MAKING OF AN
UNLIKELY ROCK STAR,
was published in April 2019, and it has been receiving rave five star reviews on Amazon. She has also written several articles that were published in Authority, Thrive Global, Huffington Post, and Woman's World magazines. Donna is a sought after speaker on topics related to health and wellness. She is an accomplished musician, former RN, and avid runner, hiker, climber, certified yoga teacher and yoga therapist.

Other Books By Donna F. Brown

If you had a second chance to follow your dreams, would you? When Donna F. Brown stepped into a garage in Chicago that fateful summer day in 1973 to audition for a hard rock band called Medusa, she had no idea what the universe had in store. With only a handful of 45's, the only reproduction of the band's existence, their music eventually found its way from obscurity into the annals of rock music history and worldwide acclaim.

"Donna F. Brown's Finding Medusa takes you on a historical journey through the turbulent sixties in Chicago, the music, the drugs, as well as a personal journey through her darkest and brightest moments.

From first co-founding the Chicago based rock group, Medusa, and waiting 40 years for the release of their LP, First Step Beyond, Medusa finally secured a place in music history. The second incarnation of Medusa1975 produced the new album Rising From The Ashes, and led to several tours.

At the heart of Finding Medusa is a story of resilience and survival. With adept control of the pen, Donna F. Brown shares intimate details of a 40-year journey in a memoir that records important events of the '60s she experienced, including the 1968 Democratic Convention riots in Lincoln Park in Chicago, in which she saw friends and strangers alike, lying beaten and bloody. She takes the reader through her experiences with drugs, the rock scene in Chicago in the 1970s, run-ins with authority, her difficult home life, a nursing career, her training as a mime with Marcel Marceau, and ultimately a return to Medusa and the music where it all started.

Finding Medusa may make you laugh or make you cry, but you will most likely find, in Donna's story, deep connections to your own."

Rick Wamer – Publisher, A3D Impressions, Inc.

www.ingramcontent.com/pod-product-compliance
Lightning Source LLC
Chambersburg PA
CBHW061153210726
48294CB00006B/1665